Best Friends

Best Friends

A Collection of Classic Stories

Featuring the Paintings

of

THOMAS KINKADE

Vignettes and Border Art by Kevin Burke

Stories and Adaptations by
Jean C. Fischer

www.tommynelson.com

A Division of Thomas Nelson, Inc.
www.ThomasNelson.com

Library of Congress Cataloging-in-Publication Data available

Best friends : a collection of classic stories / stories and adaptations by Jean C. Fischer ;
featuring the paintings of Thomas Kinkade ; vignettes and border art by Kevin Burke.
   p. cm.
  Summary: A collection of stories that describe different kinds of friendship, taken
from familiar novels and from the lives of such people as Harriet Tubman and Helen
Keller.
  ISBN 1-4003-0032-0
  1. Friendship—Literary collections. [1. Friendship—Literary collections.] I. Kinkade,
Thomas, 1958– ill. II. Fischer, Jean, 1952– III. Burke, Kevin, 1957– ill. IV. Title.
PZ5 .F54 2002
808.8'0353—dc21   2002016622

Printed in Belgium
02 03 04 05 06 SPL 5 4 3 2 1

Table of Contents

Diana Comes for Tea

ADAPTED FROM L. M. MONTGOMERY'S NOVEL *Anne of Green Gables*

*Forgiveness is the fragrance the violet sheds
on the heel that has crushed it.*

—MARK TWAIN

*Anne Shirley was a thin, red-headed girl who liked to talk a lot. In the early 1900s, she
lived on Prince Edward Island, off the East Coast of Canada. Anne didn't have a mother
or father; instead, she lived with Matthew and Marilla Cuthbert, who were brother and
sister. Since they were getting up in age, they had adopted Anne to help them on their
family farm, called "Green Gables."*

Left: The Blessings of Autumn

October was a beautiful month at Green Gables. The birches in the hollow turned as golden as sunshine, the maples behind the orchard were royal crimson, and the cherry trees along the lane put on the loveliest shades of dark red and bronzy green.

"Oh, Marilla," Anne exclaimed one Saturday morning as she came dancing in with her arms full of branches filled with gorgeous leaves. "I'm so glad I live in a world where there are Octobers. Look at these maple branches. Don't they give you a thrill—*several thrills*? I'm going to decorate my room with them."

"Messy things," said Marilla. "You clutter up your room with too much out-of-doors stuff, Anne. Bedrooms were made to sleep in."

> "You clutter up your room with too much out-of-doors stuff, Anne. Bedrooms were made to sleep in."

"Oh, and to dream in, too, Marilla!" Anne said dramatically; Anne was always overly dramatic. "One can dream so much better in a room where there are pretty things. I'm going to put these branches in the old blue jug and set them on my table."

"Mind you don't drop leaves all over the stairs then," Marilla scolded, then added, "I'm going to a meeting of the Ladies Aid Society this afternoon, Anne, and I won't likely be home before dark. You'll have to get Matthew's supper. He'll be late today, since he's hauling potatoes to the *Lily Sands*. You can ask Diana to come and spend the afternoon with you, if you'd like. The two of you can have tea."

"Oh, Marilla!" Anne clasped her hands. "How perfectly lovely! You *are* able to imagine things after all or else you'd never have understood how I've longed for this very thing. It will seem so nice and grown-uppish. Can I use the nice rosebud-spray tea set?"

"No, indeed! You'll put down the old brown one. You can open up the little yellow crock of cherry preserves, and you can cut some fruitcake and have some of the cookies. There's a bottle half-full of raspberry cordial that was left over from the church social the other night. It's on the second shelf of the sitting-room closet. You and Diana can have it, if you like."

"I can just imagine myself sitting down at the head of the table and pouring out the tea," said Anne, shutting her eyes and imagining. "I'll ask Diana if she takes sugar! I know she doesn't, but of course I'll ask her just as if I didn't know. And then I'll offer her another piece of fruitcake and another helping of preserves, and some cordial. Oh, Marilla, it's a wonderful sensation just to think of it! May I go and invite her now?"

"You may," answered Marilla.

Even though they were best friends, the girls shook hands as if they had never met.

Anne fled down the hollow and up the spruce path to *Orchard Slope,* to ask Diana to tea. And just after Marilla left for the meeting of the Ladies Aid Society, Diana came over dressed in her second-best dress and looking exactly as it is proper to look when asked out to tea. At any other time, she would have run into the kitchen without knocking, but today she knocked primly at the front door. Anne, also dressed in her second-best dress, opened the door in a very grown-up fashion.

Even though they were best friends, the girls shook hands as if they had never met. They continued this grown-up behavior until after Diana had taken off her hat and sat for ten minutes, in a ladylike fashion, in the Cuthberts' sitting room.

"How is your mother?" Anne asked politely, just as if she had not seen

Mrs. Barry picking apples that morning in excellent health and spirits.

"She is very well, thank you," answered Diana. "I suppose Mr. Cuthbert is hauling potatoes to the *Lily Sands* this afternoon?" She already knew that he was, because she had ridden into town that morning in Matthew's cart.

"Yes. Our potato crop is very good this year. I hope your father's potato crop is good, too," said Anne.

"It is fairly good, thank you," answered Diana, continuing the polite little game. "And have you picked many of your apples yet?"

"Oh, *ever* so many!" said Anne, forgetting to act polite and grown-up. "Let's go out to the orchard and get some, Diana. Marilla says we can have as many as we like. Marilla is a very generous woman. She said we could have fruitcake, cookies, and cherry preserves for tea. But it isn't good manners to tell your company what you are going to give them to eat, so I won't tell you what she said we could have to drink—only it begins with an *r* and a *c*, and it is a bright red color. I love bright red drinks, don't you, Diana? They taste twice as good as any other color."

The orchard—with its great sweeping branches that bent to the ground with fruit—proved so delightful that the girls spent most of the afternoon there. They sat in a grassy corner in the mellow autumn sunshine, eating apples and talking as hard as they could.

Diana told Anne about how much she hated sitting next to Gertie Pye in school. Gertie squeaked her pencil all the time and it made Diana's blood run cold. And she told about how Ruby Gillis had gotten rid of all her warts with a magic pebble that old Mary Joe from the creek gave her. You had to rub the warts with the pebble and then throw it away over your left shoulder at the time of the new moon and the warts would all go

Diana poured out a whole glassful.

But Anne was too eager to hear anymore. "It's time we had tea," Anne said. And the two girls hurried off to the house.

Anne looked on the second shelf of the pantry, but there was no bottle of raspberry cordial there. Finally, she found it way back on the top shelf. Anne put it on a tray and set it on the table with a large drinking glass.

"Please help yourself, Diana," she said politely. "I don't feel that I want any right now after eating all those apples."

Diana poured out a whole glassful. She looked at its bright red color and sipped it daintily. "I didn't know raspberry cordial tasted like this, Anne," Diana said.

"Do you like it?" Anne replied. "Take as much as you want. I'm going to run out and stir the fire up. There are so many responsibilities on a person's mind when they're keeping house, aren't there?"

"Marilla makes wonderful cordial," Anne replied.

When Anne came back from the kitchen, Diana was drinking her second glassful of cordial. When Anne asked if she'd like another, Diana said, "Yes. This doesn't taste a bit like any raspberry cordial I've ever had."

"Marilla makes wonderful cordial," Anne replied. "Marilla is the best cook. She is trying to teach me to cook, but I assure you, Diana, it is no easy task. The last time I made a cake, I forgot to put the flour in. I was thinking the loveliest story about you and me, Diana. I imagined you were desperately ill with smallpox and everybody deserted you, except me. I sat at your bedside and nursed you back to health. But then I caught the smallpox and died. I was buried under the poplar trees in the graveyard, and you planted a rosebush on my grave and watered it with your tears. And you never, ever forgot me, your best friend, the one who gave her life for you. It was such a sad little tale,

Diana, and the tears ran down my cheeks as I mixed the cake, and I forgot to put the flour in—Why, Diana, what is the matter?"

Diana had stood up very unsteadily, then she sat down again, putting her hands to her head. "I–I'm awful sick," she said, "I- I have to go right home."

"Oh, you mustn't dream of going home without your tea!" cried Anne. "I'll get it right away. I'll put it on this very minute."

"I have to go *home*," Diana said thickly. "I don't *feel* good."

> "I–I'm awful sick," she said. "I-I have to go right home."

"Let me get you a lunch anyhow," Anne insisted. "A bit of fruitcake and some of the cherry preserves. Lie down on the sofa for a little while and you'll be better. Where do you feel bad, Diana?"

"*I have to go home!*" said Diana, and that was all she would say.

"I never heard of company going home without tea," Anne complained. "Oh, Diana, do you suppose that it's possible you're really taking smallpox? If you are, I'll take care of you. You can depend on that; I'll never desert you. But I do wish you'd stay till after tea. Where do you feel bad?"

"I'm awful dizzy," said Diana.

And, indeed, she walked very dizzily. Anne, with tears of disappointment in her eyes, got Diana's hat and walked her almost all the way home. Then she cried all the way back to Green Gables, where sadly she put the rest of the raspberry cordial back into the pantry and got supper ready for Matthew.

⌒

The next day, Sunday, it rained from dawn until dusk, so Anne didn't go outside at all. But Monday was a beautiful day, and Anne went about her usual routine. In the afternoon, Marilla saw her running up the lane with tears rolling down her cheeks. Anne dashed into the kitchen, past Marilla, and she flung herself facedown on the sofa in the sitting room.

"Whatever has gone wrong now, Anne?" asked Marilla.

No answer came from Anne, who was crying harder than ever.

"Anne Shirley, when I ask you a question, I want to be answered. Sit up this very minute, and tell me what you are crying about."

Anne sat up with tears streaming down her cheeks. "Diana's mother is in an awful state," Anne wailed. "She thinks that I got Diana *drunk* on Saturday. She says that I must be a thoroughly bad and wicked girl to have let Diana drink something so bad. And she's never, ever going to let Diana be my friend again. Oh, Marilla! I'm just so overcome with sadness."

"Whatever has gone wrong now, Anne?" asked Marilla.

Marilla stared in amazement. "Drunk!" she said when she found her voice. "Anne, are you or Mrs. Barry crazy? What on earth did you give her?"

"Just raspberry cordial," sobbed Anne. "I never thought that raspberry cordial would make a person drunk. Not even if they drank three big glassfuls, like Diana did."

"Show me the bottle," Marilla said. So Anne took her to the pantry. And when Marilla saw the bottle, she recognized it as a bottle of currant wine that she kept only as medicine for when someone was sick. And just then Marilla remembered she had put the bottle of raspberry cordial in the cellar instead of the pantry as she had told Anne.

"Anne, you certainly have a way of getting yourself into trouble," Marilla said. "You gave Diana currant wine instead of raspberry cordial. Didn't you know the difference?"

"I never tasted it," said Anne. "I was only trying to be a good hostess. And then Diana got so very sick. And Mrs. Barry said that Diana was sick all day yesterday with the most awful headache, and she missed school today because she still felt bad. Mrs. Barry is so angry with me, Marilla. She will never believe that I didn't do it on purpose."

"She should punish Diana for being so greedy as to drink three whole glassfuls of anything," said Marilla shortly. "Why, three of those big glasses would have made her sick even if it had only been cordial—There, there, child, don't cry. I can't see as you were to blame, though wine can be a very bad thing and children should never drink it."

"I *must* cry!" said Anne. "My heart is broken. I've lost my very best friend. Oh, Marilla, I little dreamed of this when first we swore our vows of friendship."

"Don't be foolish, Anne. Mrs. Barry will think better of it when she finds you're not really to blame. I will go have a talk with her. Don't cry anymore, Anne. It will be all right."

Marilla had changed her mind about it being all right by the time she got back from *Orchard Slope*. Anne was watching for her coming and flew to the porch door to meet her.

"Oh, Marilla, I know by your face that it's been no use. Mrs. Barry won't forgive me, will she?"

"Mrs. Barry, indeed!" snapped Marilla. "Of all the unreasonable women I ever saw, she's the worst. I told her it was a mistake and you weren't to blame, but she just simply didn't believe me."

Marilla whisked into the kitchen, very upset, leaving Anne on the porch behind her. Presently, Anne stepped out bareheaded into the chill autumn dusk, and she made her way down through the clover field, over the log bridge, and up through the spruce grove, lighted by a pale little moon hanging low over the western woods. Mrs. Barry, coming to the door in answer to a timid knock, found white-lipped, eager-eyed Anne on the doorstep.

Mrs. Barry's face hardened. She was a woman of strong prejudices and dislikes, and her anger was of the cold, sullen sort, which is always hardest to overcome. To do her justice, she really believed Anne had made Diana drunk on purpose, and she was honestly trying to keep her little Diana from further trouble by continuing a friendship with Anne.

"What do you want?" Mrs. Barry asked stiffly.

Anne clasped her hands. "Oh, Mrs. Barry, please forgive me. I did not mean to—to—*intoxicate* Diana. How could I? Just imagine if you were a poor little orphan girl that kind people had adopted and you had only one best friend in all the world. Would you intoxicate her on purpose? I thought it was only raspberry cordial. Oh, please don't say that you won't let Diana be my friend anymore. If you do, you will cover my life with a dark cloud of woe."

> "I'll never have another best friend," sobbed Diana.

Anne's speech only irritated Mrs. Barry more. She was suspicious of Anne's big words and dramatic gestures and imagined that the child was making fun of her. So she said, coldly and cruelly: "I don't think you are a fit girl for Diana to associate with. You'd better go home and behave yourself."

Anne's lip quivered. "Won't you let me see Diana just once to say farewell?" she begged.

Mrs. Barry agreed to allow Diana and Anne ten minutes to say good-bye.

"Oh, Diana," cried Anne, taking hold of her friend's hands. "Will you promise never to forget me, no matter how many best friends you have?"

"I'll never have another best friend," sobbed Diana. "I don't want to. I couldn't love another friend as much as I love you."

"You *love* me?" Anne asked tearfully.

"Why, of course I do," said Diana. "Didn't you know that?"

"I knew you *liked* me, of course," said Anne, "but I never hoped you *loved* me. Nobody has ever loved me since I can remember. Oh, this is wonderful! I love you, too, Diana," Anne hesitated for a minute. "Diana, could I have a small lock of your hair to remember you by?"

> Then Anne ran home, and she cried herself to sleep.

"Do you have anything to cut it with?" Diana wondered.

"Yes. I've got my patchwork scissors in my apron pocket," said Anne. Sadly, she clipped one of Diana's jet-black curls. "Fare-thee-well, my beloved friend," Anne said dramatically. "From this day on, we must be as strangers though living side by side."

Then Anne ran home, and she cried herself to sleep.

October passed at Green Gables, then November and December, and finally January came with ice and snow. Anne and Diana were still not allowed to be friends. Anne had all but given up hope. She did not believe that God Himself could do very much with such a stubborn person as Mrs. Barry.

Marilla had gone away for two days to attend a meeting, and she left Anne and Matthew to care for themselves. Anne was just coming up from the cellar with some potatoes when she heard the sound of flying footsteps on the icy boardwalk outside. Then the kitchen door flew open and Diana Barry rushed in, white-faced and breathless.

"Whatever is the matter, Diana?" Anne cried, surprised to see her friend. "Has your mother forgiven me at last?"

"Oh, Anne, come quick!" Diana said. "My little sister Minnie May is awful sick with the croup. Mother and Father are away, and there's nobody to go for the doctor. Oh, Anne, I'm so scared!"

10

Matthew, without a word, reached out for cap and coat, slipped past Diana, and went away into the darkness of the yard.

"Matthew will go for the doctor," Anne said. "Matthew and I are such kindred spirits that I can read his thoughts without words at all. Don't worry, Diana," Anne said cheerfully "Before I came to live at Green Gables, I helped my last guardian, Mrs. Hammond, take care of three pairs of twins. They all had the croup regularly. I know exactly what to do—just wait until I get the ipecac bottle."

The girls hurried off to the Barry house. The night was clear and frosty; big stars were shining over the silent fields, and here and there, dark, pointed fir trees stood with snow powdering their branches and the wind whistling through them.

"That little red-headed girl they have over at the Cuthberts' is as smart as they make 'em. She saved that baby's life . . ."

When they got to the Barry house, they found Minnie May feverish, restless, and breathing hard.

"She has the croup, all right," said Anne. "She's pretty bad, but I've seen worse."

Anne went right to work. She made sure that Minnie May was kept warm enough, and she gave her syrup of ipecac to break up the cough. It was well into the night when Matthew arrived with the doctor, and by then Minnie May was much better and sleeping soundly.

"I was worried," Anne admitted. "It took every last drop of the ipecac before she began to get better. You can just imagine my relief, Doctor, because I can't say it in words. You know there are some things that can't be expressed in words."

"Yes, I know." The doctor nodded. He looked at Anne as if he were thinking some things about her that couldn't be expressed in words. Later on, however, he said his thoughts to Mr. and Mrs. Barry. He said: "That little red-headed girl they have over at the Cuthberts' is as smart as they make 'em. She saved that baby's life, for it would have been too late by the time I got here."

Anne was tired from the ordeal, and she slept most of the next day. When she awoke, Marilla was home.

"Mrs. Barry was here this afternoon, Anne," said Marilla. "She wanted to see you, but I wouldn't wake you up. She says you saved Minnie May's life, and she is very sorry she acted as she did in that affair of the currant wine. She hopes you'll forgive her and be good friends with Diana again."

Anne, overjoyed, sprang to her feet. "Oh, Marilla, can I go right now?"

"Yes, yes, run along," answered Marilla.

Without even grabbing her hat and coat, Anne hurried off to Diana's house.

Later, she came dancing home in the purple winter twilight across the snowy places. Afar in the southwest was the great shimmering, pearl-like sparkle of an evening star. The tinkles of sleigh bells among the snowy hills sounded like chimes in the frosty air, but their music was not sweeter than the song in Anne's heart and on her lips.

> "You see before you, Marilla, a perfectly happy person," Anne announced.

"You see before you, Marilla, a perfectly happy person," Anne announced. "Mrs. Barry kissed me and cried and she said she was so sorry. And Diana and I had such a lovely afternoon. We had an elegant tea with fruitcake and pound cake and doughnuts, and two kinds of preserves! And the best thing, Marilla, was that Diana gave me a card with a wreath of roses on it, and the card said: 'If you love me as I love you, nothing but death can part us two.' Isn't that wonderful, Marilla? And when I left, Mrs. Barry asked me to come over as often as I wanted, and she and Diana stood at the window and threw me kisses. Do you know what, Marilla?"

"What, Anne?" Marilla asked with a brief sigh.

"I feel like praying tonight," said Anne. "I'm going to think of a special, brand-new prayer to thank God for convincing Mrs. Barry to let Diana and me be friends."

Thomas Kinkade

The Railroad to Freedom

Based on the life of Harriet Tubman

I breathed a song into the air,
It fell to earth, I knew not where;
For who has sight so keen and strong,
That it can follow the flight of song?
. . . The song from beginning to end,
I found again in the heart of a friend.

—Henry Wadsworth Longfellow (The Arrow and the Song)

Araminta Ross was born into slavery on a plantation in the state of Maryland. When she was eleven, she took her mother's name, Harriet. Harriet spent most of her childhood working for her master, Edward Brodas, who sometimes rented her out to work on nearby plantations. It was a hard life. Harriet was beaten and mistreated, and by the time she was a teenager she was thinking about freedom.

Left: Homestead House

*H*enry, a tall Black slave, bolted out of the Crossroads General Store. "Run, Harriet! Run!" he cried, pushing her aside as she stood in the doorway. Mr. Hale, the overseer—a man who worked for Master— flung a heavy lead weight at Henry. It missed and hit Harriet in the head. Everything went black, and Harriet fell to the floor.

It was weeks later when she finally woke up, lying on a bed of rags in the corner of her parents' shabby little cabin. It was months before she could walk, and she would have headaches for the rest of her life. As she lay there, Harriet remembered how badly she and Henry and all of the other slaves were treated. "Someday," Harriet said, "I'm going to see to it that nobody belongs to nobody else. It just ain't right."

> She knew that runaway slaves were beaten or killed, if they were caught.

Harriet was afraid to escape from her master. She knew that runaway slaves were beaten or killed, if they were caught. And Harriet didn't want to leave her parents, brothers, and sisters. But the day came when Master died, and Harriet worried that the new master might sell her down the river, to someone in the South, where things were much worse.

Despite all the hardships and cruelty she suffered, Harriet always knew God was with her and had a plan. Harriet felt God would help her escape to freedom.

She didn't tell anyone about her escape plans—what if they told? Like many slaves, she said good-bye to her family and friends with a song. The song was a code. If her friends listened closely to the words, they would know that she was leaving. In the darkness of night, Harriet walked past their cabins and sang:

I'm sorry, friends, to leave you,
Farewell! Oh, farewell!
But I'll meet you in the morning,
Farewell! Oh, farewell!
I'll meet you in the morning,
When you reach the Promised Land;
On the other side of Jordan,
For I'm bound for the Promised Land.

Harriet had a long journey ahead of her. She hoped that someday she would cross the border between Maryland and Pennsylvania into the "Promised Land"—the place where slaves were free.

With nothing but the moon and stars to guide her, Harriet headed north. Her mind was filled with terrible thoughts of being caught, and her heart was pounding wildly. She'd never felt so afraid, or so alone. *Oh, Lord, did I do the right thing?* All the while she listened for the slave master's dogs—dogs that were trained to hunt runaway slaves. What would she do if she heard them? They would find her for sure, and then what? Harriet followed the North Star, using it as a compass. Faith kept her going, faith that friends would be waiting to help her along the way. She trusted God that it was so.

The slaves on the plantation talked about the Underground Railroad. It wasn't a real railroad. It was a group of people who were willing to help the slaves escape north because they felt slavery was wrong. These

> Despite all the hardships and cruelty she suffered, Harriet always knew God was with her and had a plan.

people were men, women, and whole families who risked their own lives and safety to help the slaves go free. These friends hid slaves in their homes, barns, and churches, wherever it was safe. They gave them food and made sure they had the things they needed, and they helped them get to the next station—or "safe house." The slaves traveled from station to station along the railroad until they reached freedom. If Harriet was going to make it to Pennsylvania, she knew the railroad was the only way.

That first night, she trudged through the woods, not far from the road. *Oh, Lord, You're the only friend I got right now. So keep me from trouble.*

There was a White woman who lived nearby, and Harriet had heard that her house was a station on the railroad. It was several miles north of the plantation. Harriet decided to go there.

The woman was a Quaker. Quakers were peace-loving people who talked differently from most of the people in the country. They used words like "thee," "thou," and "thy," words that were strange to Harriet. And they called each other "Friends." If Harriet ever needed a friend, it was now.

She hid in the woods until the sun came up. Then she went to the White woman's ivy-covered house and knocked on the front door. The door opened, and a tall thin lady, wearing a long gray dress and a white bonnet, took one look at Harriet and looked quickly around. "Come in," she said quietly. "Thou art trembling," the woman said. "Thee has nothing to fear. I know why thou art here, and I will help thee."

The woman gave Harriet some food, as much as she wanted, on beautiful plates. As Harriet ate, the woman told her what to do to stay safe. "Thee will rest here today. I shall give thee the names of friends who shall help thee along thy way. It is north, ninety miles, that thee must travel before thee arrives in the Promised Land. Thee must travel by night and hide by day."

> If Harriet ever needed a friend, it was now.

The woman took Harriet to a barn. "Thee will be safe here," she said as she made a bed for Harriet in the hay. The quilts she lent her to sleep under were pretty. And there were no holes in the blanket at all.

"Thank you, Missus," Harriet said. "Lord bless you, Missus." She could never imagine being treated as well as this woman treated her. Slaves were often beaten and abused. But this White woman was kind. She made Harriet feel like a queen.

When darkness came, the woman returned. "It is time for thee to go," she said. "Follow the road for twenty miles to the next safe house. Travel by night in the safety of the woods." The woman described the safe house to Harriet— the next station on the railroad. She gave Harriet some bread to take with her and a slip of paper with some writing on it. "When thee arrives, and the lady asks, 'Who art thou,' whisper, 'A friend of a friend.' Then give her the piece of paper."

"I won't never forget all you done for me, Missus," Harriet said. Then she hurried off into the darkness of the woods not knowing what the next day, or even the next hour, might bring.

It was two days before Harriet arrived at the house the kind Quaker woman had described. An older woman, also a Quaker, was sewing on the porch. "Who art thou?" she asked.

> "Follow the road for twenty miles to the next safe house. Travel by night in the safety of the woods."

"A friend of a friend," Harriet whispered. Harriet gave the woman the slip of paper just as a wagon came around the bend in the road. Quickly, the woman thrust a broom into Harriet's hand.

"Sweep!" she said sharply.

Harriet didn't know what was going on, but she did as she was told. *Tricked! Have I been tricked? Am I this woman's slave?*

The wagon came closer and stopped in front of the house. "Good day," said the driver.

"Good day to you," the woman replied.

"See you got a new girl," the man said.

Harriet's heart began to race. What would the woman say? What would happen if she told, and Harriet was sent back to the new master? *Oh, Lord, please make this woman as kind as the other.*

"There's much work to be done," the woman answered.

Harriet sighed a big sigh of relief. *Thank You, Lord Jesus.*

"Aye," said the man. Then he tipped his hat and drove on.

After a while, the woman invited Harriet to come into the house. Harriet wasn't sure what to do. She didn't know if she should obey or run.

> Harriet wasn't sure what to do. She didn't know if she should obey or run.

She obeyed.

The woman told her to sit down and have something to eat. "With a broom in thy hand, thee won't be seen as a runaway," the woman said. "Thee must make people think thou art owned, otherwise thee might get caught."

Another friend!

"Thee must travel north along the Eastern Shore. Thou art frightened now, but if thee minds thy way, thee will have thy freedom soon."

"I can't even imagine it, Missus," Harriet said. "Ever since I was little I dreamed about bein' free."

When night came, the woman's husband put Harriet in the back of a wagon and he covered her with potatoes and other vegetables. He told her to be sure not to make a sound as they traveled north to the next safe house.

The potatoes on top of her were heavy, and Harriet could barely breathe. The horse plodded along throughout the night. *Clip-clop, clip-clop.* The sound of its hooves was all that Harriet heard, and that, along with the rocking of the wagon, lulled her to sleep. When she woke up, she wondered if the kind Quaker gentleman was still driving the wagon. *Am I safe? Oh, Lord, be with me. Make the man a friend.*

Just before dawn, the wagon stopped. Harriet heard a voice. "When next I stop, thee must climb out of the wagon. Run straight to the woods and keep running until thee finds an old outhouse by the water. Go inside, and hide up in the loft until a man comes to get thee tonight."

Soon the wagon stopped. "Now!" said the man. "Run!"

There was urgency in the Quaker man's voice that scared Harriet. As quickly as she could, she dug through the potatoes, jumped off the wagon, and ran toward the woods—without ever looking back. *Thank you, Mister. Lord, bless my friend—Mister Quaker Man.* She ran until she came to the water, and there at the Eastern Shore was the old outhouse. Harriet hurried inside and shut the door.

> "A friend of a friend," Harriet whispered, her voice trembling.

There were no indoor bathrooms in those days, so people went outside to a wooden shed—an outhouse—and used a toilet that was nothing more than a hole in the ground. The whole place smelled awful, but Harriet had no choice but to hide there, up in a loft, until darkness came again.

Harriet didn't feel safe in this place. What would stop someone from coming there and finding her? She waited and she prayed. It seemed like forever until nighttime came. It was a moonless, starless night. Things in the outhouse were so black that Harriet couldn't see her own hand in front of her face. *Oh, Lord! Someone is coming.* The door opened and a man whispered, "Who are you?" *What should I do? Should I answer? This man doesn't sound like a Quaker.* Again the voice whispered, "Tell me. Who are you?"

"A friend of a friend," Harriet whispered, her voice trembling.

"Then come down from there," the man said, still whispering.

Oh, Lord, don't leave me now. Harriet climbed down from the loft. A shadowy figure stood in the doorway. *Oh, Lord, be with me. Keep me safe.*

"Are—are you a friend?" Harriet stammered.

"Aye," said the man. "Not a Quaker, but a friend, nonetheless."

They walked in pitch darkness to the edge of the water where there was a rowboat. "Can you row?"

"I'm strong," Harriet answered. "I can row."

"Then take the boat straight across to the other side. Leave it up on the shore. You're on your own after that. Stay in the woods. Keep going north. After about three days, you'll cross over into Pennsylvania."

Three more days to freedom!

"Thank you," Harriet said to the man. "I won't never forget you for being my friend." Then she rowed off across the water, without ever having seen the man's face.

She felt like she was in heaven. I'm free! Oh, Lord, I'm free!

During the next few days, Harriet walked through the woods and muddy swamps and on the edge of the riverbank. On starry nights, she followed the North Star, and on cloudy, dark nights she touched the trees looking for moss. She knew that it always grew on the north side of the trees. There was never a time when Harriet felt safe. She kept listening for the sounds of the master's dogs and watching for people who might be watching her. By the time she reached Pennsylvania and crossed over into the Promised Land, she was exhausted.

Harriet rested at the edge of a woods and looked all around her. There was such a glory over everything; the sun came like gold through the trees. She felt like she was in heaven. *I'm free! Oh, Lord, I'm free!* But there was nobody there to welcome her into the Promised Land.

"I know You's with me, Lord," Harriet prayed. "I'm a stranger in this strange land. But I'm holdin' steady on You, and I know You'll see me through."

The little slave girl had grown up to be a free woman in a strange land. But the story of Harriet doesn't stop there. She never forgot the slaves she left behind or the good friends who helped her escape.

Who was Harriet? She was Harriet Tubman, one of the most famous Black women who ever lived. She went on to help more than three hundred slaves to freedom, including her own family. During the Civil War, Harriet worked as a nurse. And later she started a home for the poor. She was so famous that people from all over the world came to visit her, and she was invited to visit many different lands.

And those friends who helped her along the way? They became her best friends. They were the stationmasters and Harriet was a conductor on the Underground Railroad. And they protected her when there was a $40,000 reward for her capture. Today that would be like a million dollars!

With the help of God and her friends, Harriet was never caught for doing what she knew was right. She kept the promise she made to herself when she was a teenager: "I'm going to see to it that nobody belongs to nobody else. It just ain't right."

The Secret Garden

ADAPTED FROM FRANCES HODGSON BURNETT'S NOVEL *The Secret Garden*

*Friendship is a bridge that leads
to a garden full of flowers.*

—AUTHOR UNKNOWN

When ten-year-old Mary Lennox's parents died, she was taken from her home in India and sent to live with her uncle Archibald in his dreary old mansion on the Yorkshire moors of England. Her uncle wasn't home and he wouldn't be for many months. To greet her was Mrs. Medlock, the housekeeper. She and the other servants didn't like Mary, because Mary was so disagreeable. To make things worse, Mary was the only child on the estate, or at least that's what Mary thought.

Left: Gardens Beyond Autumn Gate

*M*ary Lennox was sullen and pouting when she arrived at her uncle's house. She didn't want to be there. She already knew she would hate living in the big, gloomy mansion. "Don't expect to see your uncle," said Mrs. Medlock. "He's hardly ever home. Don't expect people to talk to you, and don't go wandering and poking about." She showed Mary to an upstairs room where supper was on the table. "This room and the next one are where you'll live."

There were nearly a hundred rooms in the house, though most of them were closed and locked. The furniture looked like it had been there forever, and the house was dark from shadows cast by gardens and trees with long trailing branches. It was the gloomiest place you could ever imagine.

The only person who talked to Mary was Martha, the housemaid. Mary disliked all the other servants and wouldn't talk to them, either. Martha was the only one whom she might consider a friend—but Mary Lennox had no friends. She was just too cranky and ill-tempered. Martha told her about a garden on the grounds with a wall and a door that was all locked up. The garden had belonged to Mary's aunt, and her uncle had shut it up after the woman died. "He locked the door and buried the key," Martha said. "No one's been in it for at least ten years."

"He locked the door and buried the key," Martha said. "No one's been in it for at least ten years."

Mary could not stop thinking about the garden. She wandered around looking for it until, finally, she found a big stone wall covered with ivy. She could see the tops of trees above the wall, and a robin sitting on a topmost branch. He sang a springtime song as if he were calling to her. "I'm *sure* that tree is in the garden," Mary said to herself.

The robin hopped around a flowerbed near the wall. Since it was late winter, the bed was bare of flowers and there was a small pile of freshly turned earth that looked as if a dog had dug there. The robin stopped to look for a worm. As Mary watched him, she saw something almost buried in the soil. When she looked more closely, she discovered that it was an old key. "It's the key to the garden!" she exclaimed.

> It was the sweetest, most mysterious-looking place.

The robin flew up onto the garden wall and began to sing. A little gust of wind came up and swung aside some loose ivy vines that were hanging from the wall, and underneath Mary saw the knob of a door and a big iron lock! With her heart thumping, she put the key in the keyhole. It took two hands to turn it, but it did turn. Mary looked around and waited a few minutes to make sure no one was watching. Then she pushed back the door—it opened very slowly. She slipped through it, and then she was standing *inside* the garden—the secret garden in which no one had set foot in ten years.

It was the sweetest, most mysterious-looking place. The walls were covered with leafless stems of climbing roses, so thick that they were matted together. From the ground, covered with wintry brown grass, grew clumps of bushes, which were rosebushes—if they were alive. They had spread their branches until they were like little trees. There were other trees in the garden, too, and climbing roses had run all over them and swung down long tendrils, which made light, swaying curtains. There were neither leaves nor roses on them now, but their thin gray branches looked like a sort of blanket spreading over everything. It was this hazy tangle, from tree to tree, that made the garden look so mysterious. It was different from any other place Mary had ever seen.

"It's so still," she whispered. She moved away from the door, stepping softly, afraid that she might get caught if anyone heard her there. "I wonder if everything is dead. Nothing looks alive—not even a tiny leaf."

Mary knew nothing about gardening, but she did know what a weed looked like. She found a sharp piece of wood and went from place to place and dug and weeded. She soon forgot that she was doing something forbidden. Oh, how angry Uncle Archibald would be if he found her in his dead wife's secret garden! And even the servants! Mary enjoyed herself so much that she felt in a world all her own. She had a wonderful time, and she worked in the garden until it was time for dinner.

> She soon forgot that she was doing something forbidden.

During dinner, Mary asked Martha for a little place to make a garden of her own. She asked, too, for some tools to use. Of course, Mary planned to use these things in the secret garden, but she didn't tell Martha, because she wasn't sure she could trust her. There weren't many people Mary *did* trust. In fact, there was no one. Martha said her little brother, Dickon, would get whatever she wanted.

Dickon was a funny-looking boy, about twelve years old. He looked very clean, his nose turned up, and his cheeks were as red as poppies. He had the roundest and bluest eyes Mary had ever seen. And he knew all about seeds and plants and working in gardens. Mary talked to Dickon for a long time. She needed this boy's help and liked him, but could she trust him? It was a chance she had to take.

"Listen to me," Mary whispered. "I have a secret, but you must cross your heart and promise that you will not tell a soul. And if you do, I will make life most miserable for you." After Dickon crossed his heart and promised, Mary told him all about the garden.

"Oh, take me there!" he said. "I have to see it!"

Once inside the four walls of the hidden garden, and without thinking, Mary grabbed hold of Dickon's arm. "Is everything dead?" she asked.

"No," Dickon answered. "It's quite alive. There's lots of old wood to be cut out, but look here—there's new wood coming, too." He knelt down by some pale green stems peeking through the earth. "These here are snowdrops and crocuses," he said. "And over there are some daffadowndillies. It's a grand garden, it is. It just needs some waking up."

Being quiet so they wouldn't be found out, Dickon started working and Mary helped with her fork and her trowel. Before long, they were talking as if they had known each other forever. As the robin watched from the treetop above, they made clearings and whispered about planting seeds, which Dickon promised to get.

"This is the best fun I ever had in my life! I'll come and help you every day," Dickon said.

Perhaps for the first time in her life, Mary felt cheerful. "I like you, Dickon," she told him. "Do you like me, too?" Mary surprised herself when she asked. To ask someone if he liked her was something Mary had never done before. She was afraid to hear his answer.

> "Is everything dead?" she asked.

"I like you wonderful," Dickon answered. "And so does the robin, I do believe."

So every day Mary and Dickon met in the garden, and they worked very hard to wake it up.

Late one night, Mary heard a strange, crying sound coming from the end of a long corridor. She did what she had been told not to do—she went wandering and poking about. Following the sound, she quietly made her way down the corridor, then to the left, then up two broad steps, and then to the right. There she saw a door. Mary walked to it, pushed it open, and entered a room.

It was a big room with old, handsome furniture in it. There was a low fire glowing faintly on the hearth and a night-light burning by the side of a carved fourposter bed, and on the bed was lying a boy, crying fretfully.

Mary crept across the room with a candle in her hand, and the light attracted the boy's attention. He turned his head on the pillow and stared at her. His gray eyes opened so wide that they seemed too big for his face. His face was sharp and delicate, the color of ivory, and he also had a lot of hair, which tumbled over his forehead. He looked like a boy who was ill, but he was crying more as if he was tired and cross than as if he was in pain.

"Who are you?" he asked in a half-frightened whisper. "Are you a ghost?"

"No, are you?" Mary asked, her heart pounding ever so hard.

"I'm Colin," the boy said. "And this is my house. What are *you* doing here?"

"I'm Mary. This is my uncle's house. And *I* live here!"

As it turned out, the boy was Mary's cousin and he was about ten years old. Colin had been lonely and sick for most of his life, and when he wasn't in bed he was in a wheelchair. The two cousins talked throughout the night and afterward met daily. Mary wanted to tell Colin about the garden, but she wasn't sure what he would do. If he told the servants, they would lock Dickon and Mary out, or worse. One day, when Colin was particularly sad, Mary decided to take a chance and tell him about the garden. "I know of a secret garden that belonged to your mother," she said in almost a whisper. For a long moment there was silence. Maybe she'd made a mistake.

> "Are you a ghost?" "No, are you?" Mary asked, her heart pounding ever so hard.

Colin smiled. Then he asked: "A secret garden?"

"After your mother died, the door to her garden was locked and the key was buried."

"Who locked it? Where was the key buried? What sort of garden is it?" Colin asked question after question.

"Your father locked it and buried the key. And he said no one should go in it ever again."

"May I see it?"

"I don't know. Aren't you too sick to leave the house?" Mary asked.

"I don't think I shall live long," Colin answered. "All of my life, I've heard people say that I shan't."

Mary noticed a picture of a girl with a laughing face. She had bright hair tied up with a blue ribbon, and her lovely eyes were exactly like Colin's.

"That is my mother," Colin said. "I don't see why she died. Sometimes I hate her for doing it. If she had lived, I believe I would not have been sick. I dare say I should have lived, too. And my father would not have hated to look at me. I dare say I should have had a strong back. . . . But I would like to see that garden. Do you think you could take me there tomorrow?"

"Your father locked it and buried the key. And he said no one should go in it ever again."

"What if the servants see us wheeling you there in your wheelchair? Or worse, what if your father sees us?" Mary asked.

"You mustn't worry," Colin said. "My father is away, and when he's gone, I am the master of this house. If I tell the servants they are to stay away from the long walk by the garden walls, then that's what they will do. If not, I will see to it that they lose their jobs."

The next day, Mary told Dickon about Colin and asked him to help her move Colin to the secret garden. And since Colin had ordered the servants away, no one noticed as they wheeled him there.

Colin looked 'round and 'round. Over walls, and earth, and trees, and swinging sprays, and tendrils, a green veil of little leaves had crept. Everywhere crocuses bloomed in gold, purple, and white. Something seemed to awaken inside Colin as he looked at what had been his mother's favorite garden. He could almost feel her there watching him. It felt good to be that close to a mother he had never known.

The sun felt warm on Colin's face, and suddenly he *looked* different. A pink glow of color crept all over him. "I'll get well!" he cried out. "My mother is here in this garden! I've seen spring now, and I'm going to see summer. I'm going to help you make everything grow here, and I'm going to grow here, too! I think I'm going to live forever! . . . I will come back tomorrow, and the day after, and the day after, and the day after," he said.

"I'll get well!" he cried out.

"Two lads and a lass just looking at springtime and watching a garden wake up," said Dickon.

"Friends," Colin said.

"Friends," Dickon said.

"Friends," Mary said.

And indeed, in the following months, oh, the things that happened in that garden! Mary, Dickon, and Colin planted seeds, and Mary and Dickon tended the beds. Colin sat in the fresh air and sunshine and watched things grow—and every day he could do a little more without being tired.

"I think," said Mary, "that this is the grandest time I have ever had."

"Even more grand than India?" asked Dickon.

"I was alone in India," Mary answered. "It wasn't any fun at all. What makes this so grand is you and Colin. Nothing is fun without best friends to share it with."

And the best friends brought the garden back to life. The robin built his nest in the tree. And green stems pushed their way through the earth, in the grass, and even in the cracks of the walls. The stems made buds, and the buds opened up to show beautiful colors—every shade of blue, every shade of purple, every tint and hue of crimson. The seeds grew to be flowers. And the roses! Rising out of the grass, tangled around tree trunks and hanging from branches, climbing up walls and spreading over them with long garlands falling in cascades. It was more beautiful than Mary, Dickon, and Colin had ever imagined. "I didn't think I'd ever see it," Colin said. "Or have such friends as you."

Something very fine had happened in the garden. Friendship bloomed along with the flowers.

Then one day Colin yelled out, "Mary! Dickon! I'm going to walk. Come here and help me." Mary stopped pruning and Dickon dropped his shovel, and they ran to Colin's side. Colin got up from his wheelchair. "I'm standing!" he cried. "And I'm going to walk over to that tree." With his friends steadying him, Colin walked. "I knew I could do it," he said. "I knew I would get strong with you here to help me." Each day, Colin became stronger. Eventually, he wasn't even sick anymore, and not only could he walk by himself, he could run as fast and work as hard as Mary and Dickon.

Summer turned to fall and the garden remained the friends' secret.

Archibald Craven felt as if he were being drawn back to the place he had so long forsaken, and he did not know why. As he drew near to it, his step became still more slow. Ivy hung thick over the door. No human being had passed that portal for ten lonely years—and yet inside the garden there were sounds. They were the sounds of running, scuffling feet seeming to chase 'round and 'round under the trees. They were strange sounds of lowered, suppressed voices—exclamations and smothered joyous cries. It seemed actually like laughter, the uncontrollable laughter of children who were trying not to be heard. And then came the uncontrollable moment when the sounds forgot to hush themselves. The feet ran faster

"Nothing is fun without best friends to share it with."

and faster—they were nearing the garden door. Then the door in the wall flung wide open, and out burst a boy. Mr. Craven reached out just in time to catch the intruder!

He was a tall boy and a handsome one. He was glowing with life and his running had sent splendid color leaping to his face. He threw the thick hair back from his forehead and lifted a pair of strange gray eyes—eyes full of boyish laughter and rimmed with black lashes like a fringe. It was the eyes that made Mr. Craven gasp for breath. "Who—What? Who!" he stammered.

It seemed actually like laughter, the uncontrollable laughter of children who were trying not to be heard.

"Father," the boy said, "I am Colin!"

Mr. Craven's soul shook with unbelieving joy. He put his hands on both the boy's shoulders and held him still. Mr. Craven dared not even speak for a moment.

"I'm going to live forever and ever and ever! It was the garden that did it—and Mary and Dickon."

"Take me into the garden, my boy," he said at last. "And tell me all about it."

They each told Mr. Craven their stories about how they met, jokes on each other, games they played, how they woke up the garden, and how Colin had become healthy.

And Mary, who had thought she was alone in the world, now had her best friends Dickon and Colin, who loved her so much. Mary, who had always been sour and disagreeable, sang songs now and laughed and played. And she smiled all the time instead of wearing a frown.

And Dickon—he was probably the happiest of all. He had never had any friends his own age, let alone *best* friends.

What a happy summer it had been.

The robin sang high in the treetop. The sun shone brightly in the sky. And all the flowers danced in the breeze.

"Let's make a pact," Dickon said. "Let's be best friends for forever and a day." And with the three friends joining hands, the secret garden sealed their friendship.

"Let's be best friends for forever and a day."

Teacher

BASED ON THE LIVES OF HELEN KELLER AND ANNE SULLIVAN

My friends have made the story of my life.
In a thousand ways they have turned my
limitations into beautiful privileges.

—HELEN KELLER

Imagine not being able to see or hear anything. That's how life was for Helen Keller. In 1882, when she was nineteen months old, an illness stole Helen's ability to see and hear. Soon she had forgotten the sounds of everything she had heard—even her mother's voice. Helen was a rebellious spirit locked in a dark world of silence, and she was alone. But all of that was about to change.

Left: Home Is Where the Heart Is II

*H*elen Keller sat at the bedside of her sick friend, holding her friend's hand and remembering the day many years before when they had first met . . .

It was March 3, 1887, and Helen was almost seven years old. She was living with her family in Tuscumbia, Alabama, in a big house called Ivy Green. Five years earlier, an illness had robbed Helen of both her sight and hearing. She was still able to sense things, but she could not communicate with the outside world. Her world was narrow, small, and dark as the blackest night.

The day had been uneventful, although Helen sensed that something unusual was about to happen. Her mother hurried around as if preparing for company, and Helen was left to fend for herself. In the early evening, Helen and her parents, Captain Arthur and Kate Keller, hurried out onto the front porch. Soon Helen felt the wood floor tremble as footsteps came toward her. *It's Mother,* she thought. She stretched out her hand, only to have it taken by a stranger. Then the stranger tried to hug her! *I don't like this at all!* Helen quickly pulled away and found the safety of her mother's arms. She knew she would not like this person!

> She stretched out her hand, only to have it taken by a stranger.

Unbeknownst to her, Helen had just met Anne Sullivan—a young teacher. Helen's parents had hired Anne to tutor Helen. Helen's father hoped Helen might learn some manners; Helen's mother hoped Helen might be able to learn even more. Both suspected it would be a miracle if Helen could just learn manners and possibly how to dress and feed herself.

Anne wanted more. She wanted to free Helen from her dark world. And she was perfect for the task. Anne understood Helen's world, because she was nearly blind until an operation restored a portion of her sight. She had spent most of her childhood in an orphanage. Her best friend had been her brother, but he had died when they were both young. Despite the hardships life had slung her way, Anne had challenged her own disabilities and succeeded in school. And she was determined that Helen would succeed, too.

Those first days, Helen was very naughty to Anne. She tried to chase her away by pinching and slapping her. She pulled a chair out from under her, and even knocked out two of Anne's teeth. But to Helen's amazement, Anne was just as stubborn.

> She wanted to free Helen from her dark world.

Each of Helen's acts only made Anne more determined to reach Helen. So, over and over, she tried to communicate with Helen by spelling words into Helen's hands, using a special alphabet for the deaf.

One day at the family water pump, everything changed. Anne pumped cold water over one of Helen's hands and spelled the word *W-A-T-E-R* into her other hand. *This means something*, Helen thought. Suddenly, she understood: *Everything has a word!* Helen pointed to Anne. Quickly, Anne spelled the word T-E-A-C-H-E-R into Helen's hand. It became Helen's nickname for Anne. She would always call her Teacher.

Helen was very smart and eager to learn. Before long, Helen and Teacher were having conversations by spelling into each other's hands. Teacher taught Helen's family how to talk to her by spelling into her hands, but most of the time Teacher acted as the translator. Teacher's hands were often very tired from spelling.

Helen learned to read books in Braille, a sort of "code" that is felt with the fingers through raised dots that stand for letters. She also learned to write by using a special wooden box that kept her letters straight. Now that she could communicate, Helen's interests were becoming like those of any girl her age.

In that first year with Teacher, Helen learned a lot, but there was still much more to learn. The two were becoming famous. The whole world was watching the things Helen was able to accomplish with the help of Teacher. Hope was given to other parents of children who were blind or deaf. The world was learning with Helen.

> The two were becoming famous. . . . The world was learning with Helen.

Teacher and Helen took long walks. They usually went along a dirt road that wound through the woods to a place called Keller's Landing on the banks of the Tennessee River. It was there that they had their best talks. One day when she was almost eight, Helen sat close to Teacher on the riverbank and took her hand to spell into it: "Are you happy that you came to live with me?"

"Yes," Teacher spelled. "When I found you, I found my best friend."

That made Helen happy, for she had never, ever had a best friend.

"We've been invited to go on an adventure," Teacher said as they sat only a few feet from the rushing river. "The great inventor Alexander Graham Bell has invited you and me and your mother to visit him in Washington, D.C. While we're there, we'll visit the White House and the President of the United States. After that, we can spend some time at the Perkins Institute for the Blind, in Boston, where I went to school. And then we can swim at the seashore!" Teacher said. "Would you like that?"

"Can we go by train?" Helen asked. She loved riding on trains and feeling all the bumps and rattles as the cars moved along the tracks.

"Absolutely!" Teacher answered. "Helen, you are becoming quite well known. Everyone wants to meet you!"

"Oh, Teacher," said Helen happily. "We'll have such a good time. Of course, no one we meet can fingerspell, so you and I can share secrets. You can tell me if someone's nose is as long as a banana or if something disgusting is stuck in someone's beard!"

But Helen was wrong. Dr. Alexander Graham Bell, the man who invented the telephone, could fingerspell. His wife and daughter were both deaf, so he was very used to spelling words with his hands. When they visited him in Washington, D.C., Helen had the most wonderful time. Dr. Bell told her a story about lions, tigers, and elephants,

"One day soon," he said, "you and I will go exploring together."

"And when people recognize us as being very famous, we'll play follow the leader," said Helen. "We'll lead all the people into the funniest places, and all the time they won't know that it's a game!"

"You behave yourself when you visit the White House," Dr. Bell said jokingly. "No tricks or pranks when you meet the President. Do you promise?"

"I promise," Helen answered, crossing her heart.

Helen's visit with President Grover Cleveland did not go well. When she was introduced to him, she wasn't sure what she should do, so she stood on her tiptoes and gave him a big kiss. The President was not prepared for a sloppy kiss on his cheek. Even with her poor eyesight, Teacher saw a look of shock and embarrassment on his face. Helen could tell the President was uncomfortable. *He doesn't like me,* she thought. *I must find Teacher.* Teacher could see how nervous Helen was, and she quickly rushed to her rescue. Helen couldn't wait to leave the White House and head for the seashore. She was ready for some fun.

But Helen was wrong.

Helen and Teacher had read a book about the ocean, and Helen longed to touch what the author called "the mighty sea." But her mother worried that Helen might get too close to the water and drown.

"Let her explore," Teacher said. "That's the way she learns."

So, dressed in their swimsuits, Helen, Mother, and Teacher went to the beach.

Helen ran toward the water, stopping just short of it. The ocean felt so vast and powerful, and the sand felt hot under her feet. Helen imagined a beach with white sand that looked like sugar. "Does sand taste like sugar?" Helen spelled into Teacher's hand.

"Taste it and see," said Teacher, "but only a little bit."

Helen scooped some into her hand and licked it. *Oh! It's bitter and crunchy, like the grounds of coffee.* Helen spit it out just as the waves washed farther onto the shore and tickled her toes. Slowly, she ventured into the water. By now the waves were pulling and pushing her every which way. Then, without warning, a tall wave crashed over her, tossing her upside down. All at once, her mouth filled with seawater, and she began to choke! *I'm going to drown!* Helen thought. But then she felt Teacher's strong hands pull her from the mighty arms of the sea, and everything was right again.

"Does sand taste like sugar?"

"Who put salt in the water?" Helen spelled as she recovered in the safety of Teacher's arms. "The water tasted salty."

"All ocean water is salty," Teacher answered and then started to help Helen dry off.

"I have a lot to learn," Helen replied, shivering and hanging tight to Teacher.

"Whatever you want to learn, Helen, I'll help you," Teacher answered. "There's nothing that you can't accomplish, if you're willing to try."

And try, Helen did. During their visit to the East Coast, she and Teacher spent time at the Perkins Institute for the Blind. There, Helen learned to knit, do beadwork, and sculpt. Before she went home to Alabama, she had learned French and even some words in Greek. "Someday we will go to France, and I will speak French," Helen said to Teacher. "After that you and I will see the whole world."

"Your mind travels to so many places that I can't keep up," Teacher said, and Helen felt her laugh.

"You *will* keep up," Helen answered. "I need you!"

When Helen was thirteen, Dr. Bell made good on his promise to take Teacher and Helen exploring. In a way, it did take them around the world. Helen, Teacher, and Dr. Bell went to the World's Fair in Chicago. At the time, the World's Fair was the most important event on earth. People came from all over to see it. It was like a huge museum with a carnival nearby.

When they entered the fair, Helen sensed the excitement around her. She trembled with anticipation, wanting Teacher's fingers to spell faster into the palm of her hand. "There are many buildings, Helen, and big crowds. It's very noisy, with loud music and people talking and laughing everywhere," Teacher spelled. "Can you smell the cows, pigs, and horses in the stock pavilions?"

"I smell dill pickles!" Helen said. "Is that what the animals eat?"

"Oh, Helen," Teacher answered. "It's the funniest thing. We're standing by a big map of the United States made entirely of pickles."

> "Your mind travels to so many places that I can't keep up," Teacher said, and Helen felt her laugh.

Helen laughed hard at the thought of a country that you could eat. All the while she held tight to Dr. Bell's arm so that she wouldn't get lost. Then he grabbed her by the hand and spelled, "People are watching. We've been recognized! Follow the leader." Hand in hand the famous trio slithered through the crowds like a snake.

They wandered through the exhibits, and Helen was allowed to touch the most delightful things: diamonds from South Africa, rare works of art, bronze statues from France. But she stopped when Teacher suggested that she touch an Egyptian mummy. "I love feeling all of these things," Helen said. "But I think it's better to leave the mummy to my imagination."

"Then enough of this!" Dr. Bell exclaimed. "It's time to ride on the Ferris wheel."

"Oh, no!" said Teacher. "It's too high!" But before she knew it, Helen grabbed Teacher's hand and pulled her up into the chair.

> "Then enough of this!" Dr. Bell exclaimed. "It's time to ride on the Ferris wheel."

Helen sat in the middle, and as the wheel went higher and higher, Dr. Bell's fingers explained everything that he saw, including Lake Michigan—which was like a vast blue sea. His fingers flew across the palm of Helen's hand, and her heart pounded with excitement as the wheel went 'round and 'round.

The more they explored the fair, the more Helen felt as if she were traveling the world. "Teacher, I want to learn to speak," she said. "I want to travel to France, and when the people ask, 'Parlez-vous Français?' I want to answer, 'Oui, Monsieur' or 'Madame,' and I want to say it with my own voice."

Dr. Bell suggested that Helen go away to a school where she could learn to speak. The thought of leaving home made Helen sad, but the Wright-Humason School in New York specialized in teaching the deaf to speak, and Helen wanted to speak more than anything else.

"Will you come with me if I decide to go?" she asked Teacher.

"Best friends stick together," Teacher answered. "Wherever you go, so will I—forever."

The following year, at only fourteen, Helen left home and went away to school. Teacher went with her. Helen studied foreign languages, geography, and arithmetic. She took speech and lipreading, and even singing lessons. But Helen couldn't hear speech! She had to imagine what the words might sound like. Learning to speak was hard. And as much as she tried she still spoke haltingly and in a monotone, gravelly voice. Sometimes she was difficult to understand.

Helen studied hard, and Teacher had much to do, too. She attended all of Helen's classes, translated anything that was spoken, and sometimes, when a Braille textbook was not available, Teacher had to spell the entire book into the palm of Helen's hand.

As busy as she was, Helen still found time for friends and parties. There was no doubt in anyone's mind that Helen was becoming a beautiful young woman. When she tried on her first party dress with its low neck and short sleeves, she felt very grown-up.

One day it was time for Helen to make a big decision: What did she want to do with her life?

"I want to go to college," she said. "But not unless you go with me, Teacher. You're my best friend, and I need you."

"It will be difficult for you," Teacher commented. "The other students can see and hear, and you will have to study harder than you ever have."

"We can do it," Helen said. "We can do anything as long as we're together."

> "Best friends stick together," Teacher answered.

Teacher helped Helen learn German, Latin, English, history, astronomy, physics, algebra, and geometry! Then Helen did something unthinkable for a blind and deaf person of her time. She took the college entrance exams. Newspapers were covering the event. The whole world was watching her! And the pressure was immense. Everyone wanted to see if the famous blind and deaf girl would go to college.

The college insisted that Teacher not be allowed in the room with Helen, and a person from the college interpreted the tests. It was hard for Helen to always understand what he was spelling, because everyone's style of finger-spelling letters is a little different. That made the exams more difficult for Helen, and she felt very nervous as she typed out her answers on a Braille typewriter.

Helen passed the exams and became a student at Radcliffe College, a famous school where all the other students could see and hear. And several years later Helen graduated with honors. The world had watched Helen grow up, learn to speak, and attend college. The world was amazed at what Helen had accomplished, and wondered: What would she do next?

> For the next forty-nine years, Helen and Anne remained best friends. . . .

Helen decided to dedicate her life to helping blind people. Teacher—her best friend and mentor—agreed to also dedicate her life to helping blind people. For the next forty-nine years, Helen and Anne remained best friends and saw each other through many of life's celebrations and tragedies. Teacher married, but despite proposals of marriage Helen chose to remain single. The two became even more well known for their worldwide efforts to help the blind. Helen wrote books and presented speeches. She and Teacher made many friends as they traveled throughout the world. They met presidents, movie stars, writers, celebrities, and royalty. And yes, they did go to France, where Helen spoke French using her own voice!

How unlikely it was that the little blind and deaf girl, whom the world never expected to be able to even feed and clothe herself, and the orphan who became her teacher would each grow up to change the world. But that's exactly what happened! Helen Keller and Anne Sullivan changed the way the world thought of and treated blind and deaf people. Their dedication and stubbornness made the world a better and more compassionate place.

As Helen remembered all of the wonderful times she shared with Teacher, she began to cry—because now her teacher and best friend, Anne Sullivan, was dying.

As Helen sat at Teacher's bedside, she felt Teacher's fingers begin to move, ever so slowly.

"Together forever," she spelled into Helen's hand. "I love you, Helen."

"And I love you, Teacher," Helen spelled back.

Thomas
Kinkade

Heidi and Her Grandfather

ADAPTED FROM JOHANNA SPYRI'S NOVEL *Heidi*

Two are better than one.

—ECCLESIASTES 4:9 (NKJV)

Alm-Uncle's house sat high on a cliff in the Swiss Alps, exposed to every wind, but also open to every ray of sunlight and with a wide view of the valley below. Behind the house stood ancient fir trees with long, thick, untrimmed branches. Farther back, the mountain with its old gray rocks rose higher still, with lovely fertile pastures and a tangle of great stones and bushes. Above them all were bare, steep cliffs. It was here, by the little house in the mountains, that Alm-Uncle often sat with his pipe in his mouth and his hands resting on his knees.

Left: Sweetheart Cottage III

*A*lm-Uncle was a fierce-looking old man with a long, bushy beard and heavy, gray eyebrows that met in the middle of his forehead like a thicket. He *always* carried a big walking stick, and he didn't speak to a single soul. He came to town just once a year, and then only for supplies. All of the townspeople were afraid of him. They talked about him in whispers, and they hid whenever they saw him coming.

He was called Alm-Uncle because he lived high atop Alm Mountain. He lived there alone, except for his two skinny goats. He kept to himself, because he was sad. His only child, a son, had been killed in an accident. And soon after, his son's wife died, leaving only their daughter, Heidi, just a baby. Alm-Uncle was too unhappy to raise his granddaughter, so he took Heidi to live with her mother's sister, a woman named Dete [pronounced DEE-tee]. With his family gone, he went up on Alm Mountain, and there he stayed, alone and angry at the world. And he never once went to see his granddaughter.

> At first, Peter was afraid of the old man.

The only one to see Alm-Uncle often was Peter, a young goatherd. It was Peter's job each morning to gather the goats from the village and bring them up the mountain to graze. Peter also picked up Alm-Uncle's goats. Alm-Uncle had nothing to say to Peter when he picked up his goats, Little Swan and Little Bear, and brought them back at the end of the day. At first, Peter was afraid of the old man. But then he got used to seeing him. It didn't matter that he didn't speak to Peter. Peter preferred it that way. He didn't know what he'd say if the Alm-Uncle was gruff with him.

⌒෮

Alm-Uncle was sitting on the front porch, smoking his pipe, when he saw Peter coming up the mountain leading the goats. By his side was a young girl, skipping and jumping merrily. Behind them was a sturdy woman neatly dressed, wearing a hat and carrying a large cloth sack. *Who might* they *be?* Alm-Uncle wondered. *I don't like visitors up on the Alm.*

The little girl was the first to reach the house. She went to the old man, held out her hand to him, and said: "How do you do, Grandfather?"

His eyes stared at the girl from under big, bushy eyebrows. "What does *this* mean?" asked Alm-Uncle roughly.

The woman reached the house just then. "I wish you good morning, Uncle. I am Dete, and I have brought your granddaughter, Heidi, to live with you. I can no longer keep her."

"*What?*" said the old man, his black eyes flashing. "What shall *I* do with a *child?*"

"That is your business," Dete said. "I must look out for myself now, and you are next of kin to the girl."

At that, Alm-Uncle stood up, and he gave Dete such a look that she took several steps backward. Then he stretched out his arm and bellowed: "Go down the mountain where you came from, and don't come back!"

Frightened, Dete quickly hurried down the mountainside. She had never heard anyone be so cross.

As soon as Dete had disappeared, the old man went back to his bench, and there he remained seated, staring at the ground without uttering a sound, while thick curls of smoke floated upward from his pipe.

While this was going on, Heidi was exploring. She found the goats' shed near the house, and she peeped into it to see what was inside. It was empty.

She continued her search and presently came to the fir trees behind the hut. A strong breeze was blowing through them, and there was a rushing and roaring in their topmost branches. Heidi stood still and listened. The sound grew fainter, and she went on again, to the farther corner of the hut, and looked

> "What does *this* mean?" asked Alm-Uncle roughly.

through one of the windows. Then she went around to where her grandfather was sitting. Seeing that he was in exactly the same position as when she left him, she went and placed herself in front of the old man, and putting her hands behind her back, stood and gazed at him. Her grandfather looked up, and as she continued standing there without moving he bellowed, "What is it you want?"

"Grandfather," she said, "I want to see what's in there."

"Come along," her grandfather said gruffly. "And bring your bundle of clothes."

Inside, there was a table and chair; in one corner her grandfather's bed; in another the fireplace where a large kettle hung; on the other side, in the wall, was a big cupboard. Grandfather opened it. Inside were his clothes, some hanging up—others, a couple of shirts, and some socks and handkerchiefs, lying on a shelf. On a second shelf were some plates and cups and glasses, and on a higher one still, a round loaf, smoked meat, and cheese. Everything that Alm-Uncle needed for his food and clothing was kept in this cupboard. Heidi looked around the room. "There's only one bed. Where shall I sleep?" she asked.

"Anywhere you like," her grandfather answered.

Heidi and her grandfather made a bed for her using straw and a heavy linen bag.

Heidi was delighted, and began at once to examine all the nooks and corners to find out where it would be most pleasant to sleep. In the corner near her grandfather's bed she saw a short ladder against the wall; up she climbed and found herself in the loft. There lay a large heap of fresh, sweet-smelling hay, and through a round window in the wall she could see right down to the valley.

"I would like to sleep up here."

"You would, would you?" her grandfather replied. "Come along, then. Help me get some straw to make your bed."

They gathered the straw without speaking, and together, Heidi and her grandfather made a bed for her using straw and a heavy linen bag. It was a fine and comfortable bed, and Heidi liked it very much.

"We have forgotten something, Grandfather," she said after a short silence.

"What's that?" he asked.

"A coverlid; when you get into bed, you have to creep in between the sheets and the coverlid."

"Oh, that's the way, is it? But suppose I have not got a coverlid?" said the old man.

"Well, never mind, Grandfather," said Heidi in a consoling tone of voice. "I can take some more hay to put over me."

She was turning quickly to fetch another armful from the heap when her grandfather stopped her. "Wait a moment," he said, and he climbed down the ladder again and went toward his bed. He returned to the loft with a large, thick sack made of flax, which he threw down, exclaiming, "There, that is better than hay, is it not?"

"That will make a splendid coverlid," she said.

With that done, her grandfather went outside and kept very busy. Heidi was quite alone until evening came. She sat on her bed, looking out the window and listening to the wind blowing through the pine trees. It sounded beautiful in Heidi's ears. Then she heard a shrill whistle, and down from the mountain came goat after goat, and Peter in the middle of them. Two lovely, thin goats—one white, the other brown—came out from the flock. They went to her grandfather and licked his hands, in which he had some salt to welcome them. Heidi ran out to see.

"Are they ours, Grandfather? Are they both ours?" Heidi cried.

"Yes, they are *mine,*" her grandfather said.

"What are their names?" Heidi asked.

"The white one is Little Swan and the brown one is Little Bear," he said gruffly.

Heidi played with the goats until it was dark, and then she realized she was very hungry. She ran to the house where her grandfather was already eating. "I would like something to eat," she said. Her grandfather didn't even look at

Her grandfather was surprised as he found himself smiling, too.

her as he shoved a plate of goat cheese, a large slice of bread, and a cup of milk in front of her.

Heidi ate it all, and then she climbed up to her bed and slept as well as if she had been in the loveliest bed of a royal princess. Later that night, her grandfather checked on her. She must have been dreaming happy dreams, for a smile was on her face. Her grandfather was surprised as he found himself smiling, too. For a moment, he thought of the happy days when his son was young, but he quickly pushed those thoughts from his mind. Then he went back to his own bed and fell asleep.

In the morning, a loud whistle awakened Heidi. She heard her grandfather's deep voice outside, and everything came back to her—where she had come from, and that now she was up on the Alm with her grandfather and no longer with Aunt Dete.

She dressed quickly and ran outside where Grandfather and Peter were waiting. "Do you want to go with Peter up the mountain?" Grandfather asked. Heidi noticed that he didn't sound as gruff.

"Yes," she said.

Quickly, Heidi washed her hands and face and ate a breakfast of bread and cheese. Then Heidi and Peter led the goats up the mountain.

It was a beautiful sunny day. The sky was a deep blue, and the sun shining on the mountain made the grass look emerald green. All around them were blue and yellow flowers. Heidi was so charmed by them that wherever she went she picked them.

Every day began that way, with Heidi and Peter taking the goats up the mountain. And every day their friendship grew. Peter told Heidi about the tiny house where he and his grandmother lived. His grandmother was blind, and they had little money, and the house was badly in need of repair.

"And the Alm-Uncle? What is it like to live with *him*?" Peter asked.

"He sounds very gruff sometimes, and he says very little. But he's good to me," Heidi said. "And I think he likes me."

And so these new friends talked and got to know one another as they went to the mountain each day. All too soon the flowers went away, the wind grew cold, and winter came. Heidi said good-bye to Peter, for he would not come in the winter when it was too cold for the goats to graze.

The days grew short, and then, one morning, Heidi looked out of the little window. It was snowing! Big flakes fell, thick and fast, until the snow came up to the window, and then still higher, until they could not open the window at all. Heidi kept running from one side of the house to the other to see how the snow was building and whether it would cover the whole house.

"Grandfather," she said, "I am worried about Peter and his grandmother. Their house needs repair. In this snowy weather, I am afraid that they might be cold and in need of help."

"Aye," grumbled her grandfather.

"She's blind, you know."

"That I know," he said.

"We should go help them," she said.

"Peter is a strong boy. He'll know what to do." There was a hint of uncertainty in Grandfather's voice.

> "Peter is a strong boy. He'll know what to do." There was a hint of uncertainty in Grandfather's voice.

"Peter can't do what you can," Heidi pleaded. "It takes tools to repair things, and they have no money for tools. But you have lots of tools, Grandfather—"

Grandfather stared at the fire in the hearth. He slowly whittled on a small piece of wood. Then he sighed, stood up, grabbed his shovel, and went outside to clear a path. When he came back in, he gathered his tools and handed Heidi her heavy wool coat. "Come along!" he said, his voice unusually soft and kind. Gently, she put her arms around him and hugged him.

"Isn't it nice to be good and kind?" Heidi asked him.

Together they climbed into a wide, wooden sled. It had a handle fastened to the side, and from the low seat Alm-Uncle could steer by holding his feet out in front against the snowy ground. Her grandfather took Heidi and placed her in his lap and wrapped her in the thick, warm blanket. He held her tight as the sled shot away down the mountain with such swiftness that Heidi thought she was flying through the air like a bird.

They went to Peter's house, and while Heidi, Peter, and his grandmother talked, Grandfather pounded and hammered all around the house. Then he climbed the narrow little staircase up under the roof and kept hammering until he had driven the last nail he had brought with him. And when it grew dark, Heidi's grandfather wrapped her in the blanket and carried her up the mountain, pulling the sled behind them.

"Isn't it nice to be good and kind?" Heidi asked him.

"Aye," the old man answered. And he found himself smiling at Heidi.

The very next day, Heidi and her grandfather again went down the mountain to help Peter and his grandmother. And so the winter passed with Heidi and her grandfather going every day to visit and work at the house. Peter's grandmother was surprised to find that Alm-Uncle was loving and kind. She said her days were no longer dreary and dark, because she had something to look forward to each day.

The townspeople noticed a change in Alm-Uncle, too. He came into town more often for supplies, and he greeted people with a nod and a pleasant "hello." They no longer feared him.

And Heidi was much happier living with her grandfather.

One night, after a long day of work and a hearty supper, Alm-Uncle sat by the hearth. "I'm glad you came to live here," Alm-Uncle said.

Heidi hugged her grandfather. "So am I, Grandfather. So am I."

He smiled warmly at Heidi. "Aye, God bless the day that you came."

Sacagawea and Jumping Fish

BASED ON THE ADVENTURES OF TWO SHOSHONI GIRLS

A friend loves you all the time.

—PROVERBS 17:17

Sacagawea and her family were traveling with other Shoshoni Indians on their way to the plains to hunt for buffalo. It would take many days to get there. Food was scarce in the mountains, and if they didn't have buffalo meat to eat, they would starve. They needed hides for warm clothing and shelter, and they needed bones for tools. Leaving the safety of the mountains was risky, but they had to do it so they could eat and stay warm when winter came. Unbeknownst to Sacagawea and her best friend, this hunt was the beginning of a series of events that would impact not only their personal lives but also the history of a nation.

Left: Lingering Dusk

*S*acagawea [pronounced Sak-uh-juh-WEE-uh] missed her home in the Rocky Mountains. She had felt safe and protected there in the shelter of the big pine trees. In the mountains she would often come out of her teepee at night and look up at the stars. The sky was so big, and the moon seemed so close that Sacagawea thought she might touch it—if only she could jump that high.

Sacagawea was a Shoshoni [pronounced Show-SHOW-nee]; the Shoshoni were a tribe of Indians that lived in Idaho. The Shoshoni were on their way to the plains to hunt for buffalo. It would take many days to get there. Leaving the safety of the mountains was risky, but they had to do it so they could eat and stay warm when winter came.

Enemy tribes lived on the prairie; tribes like the Hidatsa [pronounced hee-Dot-sah], who stole Shoshoni horses, killed their warriors, and took women and children prisoner. Every step away from the mountains took the Shoshoni closer to these dangerous people. As they walked on that hot summer day, they were very careful. Scouts went ahead to make sure the way was safe, while the rest of the tribe moved quietly across the tall, dry grass of the prairie.

> The two eleven-year-olds were best friends, and there was hardly a time when they weren't together.

The Shoshoni warriors rode on horseback, and the women and children walked. Sacagawea walked with her friend Jumping Fish. The two eleven-year-olds were best friends, and there was hardly a time when they weren't together.

"I will be happy when the hunt is over and we can go home to the mountains," Sacagawea said.

"Me, too," Jumping Fish replied. "My stomach is so empty that I could eat a whole buffalo."

60

"I could eat *two* buffalo," Sacagawea countered.

The girls laughed as they talked about who might eat the most.

"Today we will come to the Place Where the Waters Meet, and that will lead us to the plains and the buffalo," said Jumping Fish. "Then I will have a buffalo-skin blanket to warm me in the winter, a buffalo robe to wear, and new moccasins made from buffalo hide."

"Just think. We won't have to live on roots, berries, and seeds anymore," Sacagawea said. "Imagine, Jumping Fish, our stomachs will always be full—"

The girls' happy chatter was interrupted by the frantic cries of a Shoshoni scout. *"The Hidatsa are coming!"*

Sacagawea panicked and hid in a clump of bushes along the riverbank.

Sacagawea and Jumping Fish looked at one another as the Shoshoni warriors galloped off on horseback. The women and children scattered and ran for the river. Jumping Fish was lean and quick, and she outran Sacagawea. "Hurry," she called to her friend. But even running as fast as she could, Sacagawea could not catch up. She watched as Jumping Fish splashed through the water and disappeared behind a tree near a curve in the river.

The air was filled with the sound of war cries. "Fire sticks" exploded and horses' hooves thundered across the hard ground. Sacagawea panicked and hid in a clump of bushes along the riverbank. She pulled the branches tight around her head, hoping that the Hidatsa warriors wouldn't see her. The rumbling hooves came closer. Sacagawea felt a sharp tug as someone grabbed her long black hair and pulled her head backward. Before she knew it, she was thrust up onto a horse's back, and she was riding with a Hidatsa warrior. She was too scared to cry as they galloped across the prairie. Many of her people lay dead on the ground and others were running for safety. *Where was Jumping Fish?* Sacagawea wondered.

The Hidatsa warrior took Sacagawea to a place where women and children were held prisoner. Another warrior stood with a fire stick pointed at them, and the prisoners were told not to talk. Before long, Sacagawea saw a Hidatsa warrior walking toward them. Jumping Fish was with him, and she struggled as he held tightly to her arm. *Be careful, Jumping Fish,* Sacagawea thought. *Don't lose your temper.*

Altogether, fifteen Shoshoni women and children were taken prisoner that day. There was nothing their tribe could do to help them. The Hidatsas' guns were more powerful than the Shoshonis' bows and arrows.

Like the other prisoners, Sacagawea's and Jumping Fish's hands were tied in front of them, and they were forced to walk tied to a warrior on horseback. They were kept far apart so they could not talk to one another. Sacagawea watched Jumping Fish, hoping her friend would hold her temper and stay safe.

Jumping Fish was upset with herself for having been caught. She was determined to escape, when the time was right. As they walked, she memorized the route, knowing she would have to follow it to get back home. *I can do this,* she thought. *I can get away from these people.*

> Jumping Fish was upset with herself for having been caught. She was determined to escape, when the time was right.

The trail was dusty and hot. Thorny cacti grew everywhere. The thorns pierced the prisoners' moccasins and caused their feet to swell and bleed. At night they were allowed to soak their feet in the cool water of the river, but it didn't help much, because the next day there was even more cacti to walk through. The march continued for weeks, until they had gone almost one thousand miles from their home in the mountains.

It was early fall when they arrived at the Hidatsa village. Jumping Fish and

Sacagawea worked hard from dawn until dusk as slaves of the Hidatsa, but whenever they could, they found a quiet place where they could talk.

"I'm planning to escape," Jumping Fish whispered to Sacagawea. "I know the way home, and I want you to come with me."

Sacagawea's eyes filled with tears as she thought about her family in the mountains. "It's not safe, Jumping Fish. No prisoner has ever returned home. Why do you think we will?"

"Because I just know," Jumping Fish replied. "Besides, any place is better than here. Will you come?"

Sacagawea was silent. She couldn't give her friend an answer.

Several days later, a French fur trapper named Toussaint Charbonneau [pronounced Tu-SAWN Shar-bun-NO] won a card game with some Hidatsa warriors. His prize was Sacagawea. He took her as his wife. Without even being able to say good-bye to her best friend, Sacagawea had to leave the village with her new husband. She had no idea where she was going with this strange White man, except that it was even farther from home.

When Jumping Fish discovered her best friend was gone, she thought her heart would break. Now she had no reason to stay in the village. She had taken things she would need for her journey: a buffalo hide to use as a blanket, a knife, some dried buffalo meat, berries, and seeds. She had hidden them near the river in a place the Hidatsa would never

> Without even being able to say good-bye to her best friend, Sacagawea had to leave the village with her new husband.

find. There was nothing left for her to do but escape. She waited for a cloudy night so that it would be darker than usual. Then she quietly crept away from the village. Jumping Fish gathered her things and left.

The Great River stretched before her like a welcome friend. If she followed it to the Place Where the Waters Meet, she would find her way home. She had to travel quickly. Winter was coming, and it would take weeks to get back to the mountains.

On that first night, she ran for hours. She didn't even think about being tired. Her mind was set on going home and staying safe. She traveled until dawn, and then she hid in a dried-up streambed. She covered herself with leaves and branches from an old beaver dam, and she waited there until the daylight faded to darkness. She slept only a little that day, knowing that danger was not far off. Once the Hidatsa discovered she was gone, they would come after her. She was careful to cover her trail; hopefully, they would not find her.

For the first week, Jumping Fish traveled only at night, sometimes running, sometimes walking, but always moving along The Great River that would lead her home. Then one night something very frightening happened.

She heard a noise in a clump of bushes. Then in the moonlight she saw a pair of glowing eyes looking out at her. Another joined that pair and another until Jumping Fish found herself standing only twenty yards from a pack of hungry wolves.

Jumping Fish knew better than to run. She stood still, knowing that the only way to save herself was to give the wolves the dried buffalo meat she'd brought for her journey. Without it, she might starve. At this time of year, there was little to eat. The ground was cold and hard, and most of the plants were dead. But she had no choice. She took the buffalo meat from inside a little pouch she'd made in the buffalo hide. With all her might, she threw it into the pack of wolves. They pounced on it, and Jumping Fish ran. She ran faster than she had ever run before, and she didn't stop running until she was sure that the wolves were not after her. Her heart was racing and she was out of breath. She fell to her knees on the riverbank, and there Jumping Fish gave thanks that she was safe from the wolves.

The following weeks were hard ones. Jumping Fish was carefully traveling by day, not wanting to meet up with any more wolves in the dark. There was little to eat. One day she caught some small fish she saw swimming in the river. There weren't many at this time of year, and she was lucky to have found them. They made several meals. But there were many days that she went hungry.

On the twenty-first day of her journey, Jumping Fish arrived at the Place Where the Waters Meet. The mountains were not far away, and soon she would be home. It was almost dark out, so she made camp near some thickets by the riverbank. It was a beautiful November night. The sky was clear and the stars sparkled like diamonds. As she lay there trying to sleep, Jumping Fish thought of her friend Sacagawea and about how she loved to look at the stars. What had become of her best friend? she wondered. Would she ever see her again?

Snow swirled around her.

She was awakened that night by a howling wind. Snow swirled around her. She hoped that it was not The Great Snow, which would make travel impossible. She lay awake, covered with her buffalo hide, waiting for morning to come. By daybreak, there were several inches of snow on the ground.

She wrapped the buffalo hide around her and walked. The snow came up to her ankles and filled her moccasins. Her feet were frozen and numb.

There were fresh tracks in the snow—horse tracks and human footprints. What if it was the Hidatsa? It was in this place that they had captured her three months before. But the tracks were going west toward the mountains. Her people might have made them. She knew she was in great danger now because wherever she went, her footprints followed her. She did her best to walk in the footprints that were left before her. If anyone was following, they would not know she was traveling alone.

After several miles, the human tracks ended, and there were only the tracks of horses. A trail of blood led through the snow to the woods near the river. Jumping Fish backtracked and made a wide circle to the riverbank. She followed the river, being very careful and quiet. She wanted to see where the trail of blood ended. There, in the cold water, was what remained of a deer. The hide had been removed and almost all of the meat was taken from the bones.

But there was enough left for Jumping Fish. When she was sure no one was watching, she ate the raw meat until she was full. Now she knew she would be strong enough to finish her journey.

"We come in peace," Captain Lewis said.

Three days later, very tired and half frozen, Jumping Fish saw the familiar teepees of the Shoshoni people. Her mother hardly believed it when her daughter stumbled into the camp. She ran to her and hugged her and cried. Jumping Fish took a long nap near the fire and she ate a big meal. Then she told of her escape and about how Sacagawea was taken by a White man who won her in a card game.

⁓

Four years passed, and Jumping Fish had all but given up hope of ever seeing Sacagawea again, though she still wondered often about her friend. Perhaps she was no longer alive. If only Sacagawea had decided to escape with Jumping Fish, things might have been very different.

It was a hot August day when several White men walked into the Shoshoni mountain camp. One of them wore a fringed buckskin jacket and carried a peace pipe. The Shoshoni leader, Cameahwait, went to meet them. The man with the peace pipe said he was Captain Meriwether Lewis.

"We come in peace," Captain Lewis said. "We have been sent by 'The Great White Father,' President Thomas Jefferson." Lewis gave the women and children presents he brought for them, and he gave Cameahwait an American flag.

Meriwether Lewis went on to explain that he and his people were on a mission to explore the land west of the Mississippi River. They were badly in need of horses, and they wondered if the Shoshoni people might help them. Cameahwait told Captain Lewis to bring his people into the camp.

Lewis promised to return, and he went to tell his people the good news.

Among them was his partner, William Clark, along with a fur trader named Toussaint Charbonneau—and his wife, Sacagawea! In a cradleboard, Sacagawea carried their baby boy named Pomp.

As they came into camp, the tribe hurried to meet them. Jumping Fish looked hard at the woman who held the little boy. "Sacagawea!" she cried.

The two best friends ran to each other and hugged. Sacagawea explained that Lewis and Clark met Charbonneau several months before they began their journey. They asked him to come along because he knew the wilderness well. They knew they would need horses to get across the Rocky Mountains, and they planned to ask the Shoshonis for help. Since Sacagawea was Shoshoni, they wanted her to serve as an interpreter. Sacagawea had been so excited to be going home. Home! She couldn't believe she was really there.

Just then a tall, lanky man approached her. It was the Shoshoni leader. Sacagawea could not believe her eyes. The leader was her brother Cameahwait! She fell into his arms and wept.

> The two best friends ran to each other and hugged.

Jumping Fish, Sacagawea, and Cameahwait spent almost a month together in the safety of the mountain camp. Then when it was time for the Lewis and Clark expedition to leave, Sacagawea knew she had to go with them.

The two best friends shared one last hug.

"I will miss you," Jumping Fish said with tears in her eyes.

"I will miss you, too," Sacagawea said. "But remember that we are together in our hearts. When we look up at the big sky, we will think of one another, and we will be forever friends."

A Christmas Story

ADAPTED FROM LOUISA MAY ALCOTT'S NOVEL *Little Women*

Give, and you will receive. You will be given much.
It will be poured into your hands—
more than you can hold.

—LUKE 6:38

Growing up in New England, the March girls were not only sisters, they were best friends. Meg, the oldest, was sixteen, and she was very pretty. Fifteen-year-old Jo was tall and thin with a mane of chestnut brown hair that fell to her waist. Beth was a bright-eyed girl of thirteen with a shy, timid voice and a peaceful expression. And Amy, the one with blond curls, though the youngest, was the most important sister of all—at least that's what she thought. Amy had a very high opinion of herself.

Left: Home for the Evening

*C*hristmas won't seem like Christmas," grumbled Jo, lying on the rug.

"I hate being poor," sighed Meg, looking down at her old dress. "Don't you wish we had the money Father had when we were little, Jo? Then we'd be happy."

"It's not fair for some girls to have everything, and others to have nothing," complained Amy.

"But we have *a lot*," said Beth from her corner. "We've got Father, and Mother, and we have each other."

"We haven't got Father," Jo answered sadly, thinking of their father far away fighting in the Civil War. He was a chaplain, and he was busy taking care of the soldiers in the Union Army. The girls missed him very much.

"I've been dying to go and fight in the war," said Jo, who was every bit a tomboy. She held up the blue army sock she was mending. "But all I can do is stay at home and mend socks for the soldiers."

It was Beth who stopped the argument.

Nobody spoke for a minute or two. Then Meg said, "Mother thinks that we shouldn't get each other presents for Christmas this year, since it's going to be such a hard winter. She thinks it wouldn't be right to buy presents when Father and the other men are suffering in the war."

"But she didn't say anything about buying something for ourselves, did she?" asked Jo. "We each have a dollar saved. Let's buy what we want and have some fun. I've had my eye on a book down at the general store. That's what I'll spend my money on."

"I'll spend mine on some new sheet music," said Beth, who loved to play the piano.

"I'd like a box of colored pencils," said Amy.

Meg wasn't sure what she wanted. There were many pretty things she would like to have.

The four best friends sat talking and sewing, while the December snow fell quietly outside the window and a fire crackled cheerfully inside the fireplace. The room they were in was a comfortable old room, though the carpet was faded and the furniture was very plain.

Jo looked at their mother's slippers warming by the fire. "Marmee's slippers are getting worn out. She should have a new pair."

"I'll buy her some with my dollar," said Beth.

"No, *I* will, with *my* dollar," cried Amy.

"I'm the oldest!" said Meg. "I'll buy them."

"*I* will get the slippers," said Jo firmly. "Because I promised Father that I would take care of Marmee while he is away."

> It would be so good to have Father home again.

It was Beth who stopped the argument. "Let's each get her something for Christmas and not get anything for ourselves," she said.

The sisters thought about that for a while, and then Meg announced, "I'll get Marmee a pair of warm gloves."

"And I will get the slippers," said Jo.

"I'll get her some handkerchiefs," said Beth.

"And I'll get Marmee a little bottle of cologne," said Amy. "It won't cost so much, and I'll have enough money left over to buy my pencils."

"Then it's decided," Jo told them. "We'll shop for Marmee tomorrow—"

"Hello, my girls," said a happy voice at the door.

"Marmee's home!" the sisters cried, all together. And they ran to meet their mother, who had just returned from packing boxes of supplies for the soldiers.

"I have a letter from Father," Marmee said. "I'll take my coat off, and then I'll read it to you."

The girls gathered around their mother as she read the letter aloud. It was a cheerful, hopeful letter. At the end of it, Father wrote:

Give my girls a hug and a kiss. Tell them that I love them, I think of them every day, and I pray for them every night. When I come back, I will be as proud as ever of my Little Women.

Everyone sniffed when they came to that part, because they knew Father was always in danger. Jo wasn't ashamed of the big tear that dropped off the end of her nose, and Amy didn't mind that her pretty blond curls got crushed when she laid her head on her mother's shoulder and cried. It would be so good to have Father home again.

It was Jo who woke up first on that dreary Christmas morning. There were no stockings hanging on the fireplace, and for a minute she felt disappointed. She remembered a time long ago when her stocking fell down because it was so crammed with presents. Then Jo felt something under her pillow. She slipped her hand underneath and pulled out a little red book.

She woke Meg with a "Merry Christmas!" and Meg looked under her pillow to find a green book, with the same pictures inside and a note written by their mother, which made their one present very special. Then Beth woke up, and Amy, too, and they found books under their pillows. And all of them sat looking at the books while the sun rose.

Then they all dressed and hurried downstairs with the presents they had bought for Marmee. A special breakfast was set on the table: fruit, muffins, buckwheat pancakes, and freshly baked bread. It was the best breakfast they'd had in months—a fine breakfast for Christmas Day. But their mother was not there. Hannah, their longtime housekeeper and cook, said Marmee had left early in the morning to go to the Hummels' house.

Just as the girls sat down to their breakfast, Marmee came in from the cold.

"Before you start, girls, there's something I want to ask you," their mother said. "Mrs. Hummel has a brand-new baby. All six of her children are huddled into one bed to keep from freezing, because the house is so cold. There is nothing to eat over there, and they are suffering and hungry." Marmee paused before going on. "Will you give them your breakfast as a Christmas present?" she asked. "It means that we will just have bread and milk again today."

> "We're funny angels in hoods and mittens," Jo said.

By now, the March girls were very hungry, and the wonderful breakfast of pancakes, fruit, and muffins looked and smelled so good. Yet together they packed up their breakfast and off they went, hungry, into the cold to the Hummels' house.

The Hummels lived in a miserable place with broken windows, no fire in the fireplace, and few blankets on the beds. Greeting the Marches were a tired mother and a wailing baby. A group of pale, hungry children cuddled under one dirty, old quilt, trying to keep warm. But all of the children smiled and stared as the girls came through the door.

"Oh, my goodness!" cried Mrs. Hummel. "Angels have come to help us."

"We're funny angels in hoods and mittens," Jo said. And all of the Hummel children laughed.

In a few minutes, it really did seem as if angels had been at work there. Hannah, who had brought wood from home, made a fire, and she stuffed the broken windowpanes with old rags and her own coat. Mrs. March gave the mother tea and cereal and promised to help her, and she dressed the little baby as tenderly as if it were her own. In the meantime, the girls set the table with the wonderful breakfast. They sat the children down near the fireplace and fed them, one by one, as if they were hungry little birds. And as they ate the muffins and pancakes and bread, the children cried, "This is good!"

It was a very happy breakfast, even though the March girls didn't get any of it, and when they left the Hummels' house they were satisfied to go home to their own breakfast of just bread and milk.

"That was loving our neighbor better than ourselves, *and I liked it*," said Meg.

While Marmee went upstairs to collect clothes for the Hummel children, the March girls went into the living room and set out their presents for her. When they heard their mother coming, they shouted: "Merry Christmas, Marmee!" And Meg led their mother to the seat of honor in the center of the room.

Mrs. March was both surprised and touched. She smiled as she examined her presents and read the notes that accompanied them. The slippers went on at once, a new handkerchief that was well-scented with Amy's gift of cologne was slipped into her pocket, and the warm gloves were a perfect fit.

There was a good deal of laughing and kissing and explaining, in the simple, loving way that makes Christmas so special. And the rest of the day was spent having fun and enjoying one another's company.

The excitement of Christmas Day had hardly begun to go away when Hannah appeared and said, "There's a surprise in the dining room."

When the girls saw the table set, they looked at one another with amazement. It was just like Marmee to do something special for them, but anything this fine was unheard of during these days when there was so little money to spend.

The table was set with ice cream—two big dishes of it, strawberry and vanilla—and cake and a candy dish filled with chocolates. And in the middle of the table were four big bouquets of beautiful flowers, one for each of the girls.

Amy, Jo, Beth, and Meg stared first at the table and then at their mother, who looked as if she was enjoying their reactions.

"Santa Claus did it," announced Beth.

"Mother did it," answered Meg.

"All wrong," said Mrs. March. "Old Mr. Laurence sent it."

"The old man next door!" Meg squealed. "What in the world put such an idea into his head? We don't even know him. And there's that *boy* living with him. It's his grandson, I think."

"Hannah told Mr. Laurence about your Christmas gift to the Hummels, and that pleased him," explained Marmee. "He can be an odd, old gentleman sometimes, but he knew my father years ago, and he sent me a polite note this afternoon. He asked if he could send us a few treats in honor of Christmas Day. I couldn't say no, so you girls have a special treat tonight to make up for your simple breakfast of bread and milk."

By now, plates were passing around the table and the ice cream was beginning to disappear.

"The boy who lives with him is very shy. He seems nice, but he never speaks to us girls," said Amy.

"I talked to him once when the cat ran away," said Jo. "We were talking across the fence, getting along just fine, and then he saw Meg coming, and he walked away. I'd like to know him. He needs to have fun, I think."

"I like his manners, and he looks like a gentleman," said Marmee. "So I don't mind if you want to get to know him. He brought the flowers himself today, and I should have asked him in. He looked so sad when he went away."

"Well, he won't be sad for long," said Jo. "Not with the March girls as his friends."

They were all quiet then, content to enjoy the happy feast.

And so it was that what started as a dreary Christmas morning turned into a bright Christmas Day filled with friendships . . . and it ended with a happy feast and the promise of a new friend. And that was much more than the girls had ever expected.

The Flagmakers

BASED ON THE TRUE STORY OF CAROLINE PICKERSGILL

When love and skill work together
expect a masterpiece.

—JOHN RUSKIN

Caroline Pickersgill and her mother had just left the newspaper office, where her mother placed an advertisement. She was a flagmaker, and business was booming because America was at war with Great Britain. There had been fighting in other parts of the country, but so far the battles had stayed away from where Caroline and her family lived—however, that was about to change.

Left: Cobblestone Village

77

*I*t was a bustling summer day in Baltimore. It was especially busy down at the shipyard where big barges were being built and navy frigates were in port.

"Are your flags flying on those masts?" Caroline asked.

"I suppose," Mrs. Pickersgill answered.

"Will you make flags for the warships, too?" Caroline wondered.

"If I'm asked," her mother replied. "But not for the British!"

America was at war in that summer of 1813. The idea of war was new to Caroline. She wasn't born when the first war ended. Most people thought the first war had stopped the fight forever, but now there were rumors that the British were back and that their navy was attacking towns up and down the Atlantic coast. Everyone worried that Baltimore might be next. Caroline saw things and heard things that upset her. She saw men digging a big trench along the outskirts of the city. She heard them talking about gun barges being built in the harbor. Improvements were being made at Fort McHenry, only three miles away, and a big cannon was mounted there at the water's edge. All of these things made Caroline feel afraid.

It frightened Caroline to see him.

"I wish Papa were alive," she said. "If the war comes here, will we be all right without him?"

"We'll be fine, dear," her mother said. "God watches over us, and Papa does, too."

They went to the mercantile next. For as long as Caroline could remember, ever since they had moved in with her grandmother, Rebecca Flower Young, on Albemarle Street, she had gone with her mother to buy cloth. She loved to watch her mother and grandmother sew the brightly colored flags. She especially liked it when they made an American flag with big red and white stripes, and on a field of bright blue, fifteen white stars—one for each of the thirteen colonies plus Vermont and Kentucky.

Now that Caroline was thirteen, and feeling very grown-up, she asked her mother if she could help sew the flags.

"I should like that," Mrs. Pickersgill replied. "Would you like to be a flag-maker someday?"

"I want to be one now!" Caroline said. And that pleased her mother very much.

The next morning, a man in uniform came to their door on Albemarle Street. It frightened Caroline to see him. She remembered when she was five years old and a man in uniform came to their house in Philadelphia to say that her father had died in London.

"Good day," said the man who stood there now. "Might you be Mary Pickersgill, the flag-maker?" Mother said she was, and she invited the man in.

"The only thing that is missing is a flag so large that the British ships will have no difficulty seeing it from a distance."

"Permit me to introduce myself, Madame. I am Major Armistead, commander of Fort McHenry. I should like to commission you to create a flag."

The man was invited to sit down, and Grandmother brought him a cup of tea.

The military had chosen Mary Pickersgill for the task because of her ability to make flags and because Grandmother had made the Grand Union Flag that General George Washington raised over his headquarters at Cambridge, Massachusetts, on January 1, 1776.

"Let me assure you, Mrs. Pickersgill, that Fort McHenry is ready to defend Baltimore against the British, should that day come. The only thing that is missing is a flag so large that the British ships will have no difficulty seeing it from a distance. It must be an American flag with fifteen stripes in red and white. And it must have fifteen white stars on a blue background." He

79

coughed and sputtered a bit before going on. "Oh . . . and . . . ah . . . it must measure forty-two feet by thirty feet."

"Forty-two by thirty feet!" cried Mary Pickersgill. "Why, you're asking me to sew a flag that's as tall as a four-story building!"

"And we'll need a smaller flag, too, to fly in bad weather," the major continued. "That one's only seventeen by twenty-five feet."

"It will take time to do it, and the war could come here any day. How soon will you need it?" Mrs. Pickersgill said.

"We need them both in a month," the major stated.

It was deadly silent in the sitting room of the Pickersgill house. Mary Pickersgill had never sewn anything as large as a flag that might fly from a ninety-foot pole. She wasn't sure if she could make even the larger flag in a month, but could she possibly make both flags in that time? How long would it take to get the fabric and thread? She would need hundreds of yards of fabric and many spools of thread. She would have to sew day and night to finish on time. She looked at Caroline's grandmother and then at Caroline.

Finally, she said, almost in a whisper, "It seems impossible to do it in a month."

> Mr. Ellsworth's eyes widened and his jaw dropped. "Four hundred yards!" he gasped.

But Grandmother, who had much more experience as a flagmaker, didn't agree. "It's not impossible if Caroline helps us," she said. "That would make three, and we have good friends to help when we need them."

Mrs. Pickersgill hoped her mother was right. She wondered if Grandmother's old hands would be strong enough to sew night and day. And Caroline had no experience as a flagmaker. She would have to learn as they sewed. But they were very patriotic women. Their country needed them now. They had no choice but to honor the major's request. They had to try.

"We shall do it!" answered Caroline's mother. "Major Armistead, you shall have your flags."

The Pickersgill women went right to work. The first friend they went to was a merchant, Mr. Ellsworth. "Dear friend, I need your help," said Caroline's mother. "I have a very large order to place, and I shall need it filled straightaway. I will need about four hundred yards total of red, white, and blue English wool bunting and twenty-five yards of white American cotton, and enough strong linen thread to join it all together."

> "I see the need for a friend," said Grandmother.

Mr. Ellsworth's eyes widened and his jaw dropped. *"Four hundred yards!"* he gasped. But when he found out why she needed it, Mr. Ellsworth, being a very patriotic fellow, promised to fill the order right away.

"It will take me a little time to get it all," he said almost to himself as he glanced around his store. "I'll have to call on friends—other merchants—to help me complete the order. Some others may have to wait longer for their orders." Then he looked straight at Mary Pickersgill and said in a very determined voice, "I'll find it. I'll give you all that I have right now."

They had enough to start on the smaller flag. While they worked on it they were interrupted by merchants from throughout the area who were delivering bolts of fabric to the Pickersgills' door. Within a week they had finished the small flag and had enough fabric to start on the big one.

First, they cut. Mother measured the white cotton cloth, and Caroline cut out the fifteen stars, each one two feet from point to point. Next, they cut eight red stripes and seven white ones, each two feet wide and forty-two feet long. Soon the sitting room in the little house on Albemarle Street was covered with strips of red and white, and it looked like a giant peppermint stick.

"I see the need for a friend," said Grandmother. "There isn't a room in this house big enough to lay out such a flag. In fact, there isn't a house in all of

Baltimore with a room big enough. We'll need a place to stitch it together."

But where? They knew of no place big enough to lay out the giant flag.

"Go to the merchants, Caroline," her mother said. "See if any of them can help us."

Caroline was gone for hours. "What shall we do if she can't find a place?" her mother worried.

"Perhaps we can work out-of-doors if it doesn't rain and there is no wind—" Grandmother offered.

Just then, Caroline burst through the door, out of breath, with good news.

> Every night was the same. The townspeople came, and they all did their best to help.

"Mr. Claggett at the brewery says that we can use the malthouse floor, but only after the brewery closes for the night, and we have to move out by the time it opens each morning. He wants to know yea or nay."

"Quickly go and tell him 'yea,'" said Mrs. Pickersgill. "Tell him we will be there tonight. Then gather as many candles as you can, Caroline. We will have to stitch by candlelight."

That night Caroline, her mother, and her grandmother took the pieces of the flag to the brewery. There were so many pieces that it took several trips. They laid them out on the malthouse floor and marveled at how big the flag would be. They lit all the candles, but the brewery was still too dark to work in, so merchants brought more candles to help light the way. As news spread about the project in the brewery and how quickly it had to be done, people from all over town came to move the candles to give the best light as the Pickersgill women snipped and stitched. There were hundreds of candles that had to be moved inch by inch every time the women began sewing another pair of red and white stripes. Hours passed and the women were hungry, so the baker brought a basket of bread, and the grocer brought some cheese. Caroline, her mother, grandmother, and friends worked past midnight, and then they packed up the flag and carried it back to the Pickersgills', and all went home to sleep.

Every night was the same. The townspeople came, and they all did their best to help. Some brought food and candles, some moved candles, others rubbed Grandmother's tired, swollen hands whenever they got a cramp. And as the days went by, they all wondered if the great flag would be finished on time. There was so much to do, and so few hours to work in the brewery.

> "God did provide," said Grandmother. "And now may He protect us all from harm."

Slowly, the pieces of cloth were coming together. And with each stitch Caroline learned to be a flagmaker. She learned to make flat felled seams and to use tight stitches so that the enormous flag wouldn't come apart in the wind. She learned to use linen thread to join the stars to the bright blue background, and she learned to sew neatly, by hand, of course, because there were no sewing machines in those days.

After weeks of snipping and stitching, the flag was finally done. It was almost as tall as a four-story building, and it weighed ninety pounds!

"It's finished!" said Grandmother. "God bless our friends for their help."

Everyone clapped and cheered. "'Tis a grand flag," said Mr. Claggett, "a grand flag for Baltimore, and one that the British will surely see if they dare to come this way."

"We couldn't have done it were it not for your friendship," Mrs. Pickersgill said.

"Nor if Mr. Ellsworth hadn't secured the cloth for us," said Caroline, "or if our friends hadn't come to move the light and bring us food."

"God did provide," said Grandmother. "And now may He protect us all from harm."

Mr. Claggett and Mr. Ellsworth carefully folded the heavy flag and then carried it to the Pickersgill house, and in the morning, soldiers from Fort McHenry picked it up.

A whole year passed, and the war didn't come to Baltimore. Then one day, late in August 1814, Caroline heard something terrible. "Mother!" she cried as she ran through the front door. "The men say that the British are coming. They're headed for Washington, and it's only a matter of time before the war comes here!"

What Caroline heard was true. Three weeks later, British ships attacked Fort McHenry. They came in the middle of the night on September 13. Caroline, her mother, and Grandmother were awakened by the sounds of bombs.

"Mercy!" cried Grandmother as the three of them watched from an upstairs window. It was a stormy night, and lightning mixed with great arches of red fire in the sky. It was hard to tell the sound of thunder from the sounds of the bombs and the rockets. All night long the little house on Albemarle Street shook with the sounds of war. Then, in the hours just before dawn, everything became quiet.

"Is it over?" Caroline asked, praying that it was.

"I don't know, dear," her mother answered. "We'll have to wait until dawn to see if the flag is flying at the fort."

"Look!" shouted Caroline. "There's our flag!"

Someone else was watching and waiting, too—a well-known lawyer from Washington.

On the night the British attacked Fort McHenry, the lawyer was on one of the ships at sea. All at once, bombs started bursting, and he saw the red glare of rockets overhead. He watched the shelling of Baltimore throughout the night, worrying and wondering what he would see by the early light of dawn. If the American flag was flying high atop the pole at Fort McHenry, he would know that Baltimore had won the battle against the British. If it wasn't there, then he would know that the British had won.

Caroline, her mother, and Grandmother watched from their upstairs room as the lawyer watched from the ship at sea. Even when dawn came, they couldn't see the fort, because the smoke and mist in the harbor was so thick. Then, finally, the sky cleared.

"Look!" shouted Caroline. "There's our flag!"

Indeed, the flag they had made was flying at Fort McHenry. The lawyer saw it, too. It was such a beautiful flag that he had to find a way to describe what he saw. He pulled an unfinished letter from his pocket, and on the back of it he wrote a poem. Later that day, he had his poem printed, and he gave away copies all over Baltimore.

Before long, the citizens of Baltimore gathered and listened as an actor, Ferdinand Durang, sang the lawyer's poem to the tune of an old song. It went like this:

> *Oh! say, can you see, by the dawn's early light,*
> *What so proudly we hailed at the twilight's last gleaming?*

That's right! The attorney on the ship was Francis Scott Key, and it was his poem, put to music, that became *The Star-Spangled Banner.* Our national anthem might not have been written had it not been for the flag made by Caroline Pickersgill, her family, and, of course—with the help of their friends!

THE STAR-SPANGLED BANNER
by Francis Scott Key

Oh! say, can you see, by the dawn's early light,
What so proudly we hailed at the twilight's last gleaming?
Whose broad stripes and bright stars, through the perilous fight,
O'er the ramparts we watched were so gallantly streaming?
And the rocket's red glare, the bombs bursting in air,
Gave proof through the night that our flag was still there.
Oh! say, does that star-spangled banner yet wave
O'er the land of the free and the home of the brave?